# Contents

## Editorial

## Fiction

## The Quarterly Review

# Contents

# Editorial for Theaker's #46

## Stephen Theaker

Christmas time! I write this editorial at the beginning of December, which means I've just finished taking part in Nanowrimo. What an adventure! Ups, downs, procrastination, heroic efforts! And in the end I got it done, finishing a novel for the first time since 2006. Don't worry – you'll get to read it in these pages at some point.

First, enjoy what we have in this issue. I haven't read it yet, not all of it – our submission period for this issue just closed and I'm reading everything now. But I bet it's going to be great. The stories I've accepted so far have been.

The print edition of this issue (and hence the pdf version too) is in a slightly smaller format to previous issues, which I appreciate will be annoying on your bookshelves. The main goal as ever is to make production hassle-free, by making each page of proofreading a little less work to read, but that should make it easier for readers too. Another reason is to increase the likelihood of issues reaching the minimum number of pages necessary for having spine text when printing with Amazon, the absence of which has bothered some of you, and me too. Lulu used to allow spine text at lower page counts. We don't know yet how the issue will actually look – if we're not happy with it, we might go back to the old format next time.

The other change this time is to the reviews section, where all the reviews are now arranged in alphabetical order, rather than in groups. Partly this is to make the names of the items reviewed the sub-headings, which will make creating the ebook version of the magazine more straightforward. I also think it will create more variety for readers, as rather than having all my audio and comic reviews in a bunch, with all Douglas and Jacob's film reviews at the back, they'll all be intermingled.

As ever, if you have any thoughts, let us know!

If this issue doesn't leave you full to the brim with fictional goodness, don't forget that we've just published the second and last (so far as we know) of Michael Wyndham Thomas's *Valiant Razalia* sequence, which will knock your socks off.

The deadline for submissions for *Theaker's Quarterly Fiction* #47 is **28 February 2014**. We'll be reading submissions and selecting material for that issue during the first four or five days of March.

## Contributors

**Charles Wilkinson**'s short stories have appeared in *Best Short Stories 1990*, *Best English Short Stories 2*, *Midwinter Mysteries* and *London Magazine*. A collection, *The Pain Tree and Other Stories*, was published by London Magazine Editions. *Ag & Au*, a pamphlet of his poems, recently appeared from Flarestack Poets, Birmingham. Previously in *Theaker's*: "Notes on the Bone" (#41) and "Notes from the Undergrowth" (#44). This issue: "Petrol-Saved".

**Douglas J. Ogurek** reviews *The Hunger Games: Catching Fire* for us this time. His work has appeared in the *BFS Journal*, *The Literary Review*, *Morpheus Tales*, *Gone Lawn*, and several anthologies. He lives in a Chicago suburb with the woman whose husband he is and their five pets. His website: www.douglasjogurek.weebly.com.

**Gary Budgen**'s fiction has been published in a number of magazines and anthologies including *Interzone*, *Theaker's Quarterly Fiction* ("Through the Ages", #43) and *Morpheus*

*Tales*. Recently he has had stories in the anthologies *Where Are We Going?* and *Urban Green Man*. He is a member of London Clockhouse Writers. Read more at http://gary-budgen.wordpress.com. In this issue: "Black Ribbon".

**Howard Watts** is a writer, artist and composer living in Seaford who provides the fantastic cover art for this issue. In fact, he provided it over a year ago, for the issue originally intended for Christmas 2012.

**Jacob Edwards** reviews *About Time, Computing with Quantum Cats, The Day of the Doctor* and *Gravity* in this issue. His heart belongs to Australia's speculative fiction flagship *Andromeda Spaceways Inflight Magazine*, but we're happy to be his holiday romance. This writer, poet and recovering lexiphanicist's site: www.jacobedwards.id.au.

**Jessy Randall**'s stories, poems, and other things have appeared in *Asimov's, Flurb, Lady Churchill's Rosebud Wristlet, LQQK, McSweeney's*, and *Star\*Line*. Her website is http://personalwebs.coloradocollege.edu/~jrandall/. Her story in this issue: "The Night of Red Butterflies".

**Josie Gowler** specialises in writing weird tales set in the English East Anglian Fens, and science fiction and fantasy short stories; she has most fun when these all overlap. She's been published in *365 Tomorrows, Lorelei Signal, Theaker's Quarterly Fiction* ("Soldier", all the way back in #28) and *Bewildering Tales*. She is a Napoleonic re-enactor and is currently working on a trashy coming-of-age space opera. Her story in this issue is "The Lazarus Loophole".

**Mitchell Edgeworth** lives in Melbourne, Australia, and his fiction has been published in *The Battered Suitcase* and *SQ Mag*, as well as here. He keeps a blog at www.grub-streethack.wordpress.com and tweets as @mitchedgeworth. "Customs" is the fourth in his *Black Swan* series to appear in these pages. Like everything we publish, it can be read quite happily in isolation, but if you want to find out how the

*Black Swan* got off the ground, see his stories in #40 ("Homecoming"), #42 ("Drydock") and #43 ("Flight").

**Ross Gresham** teaches at the Air Force Academy in Colorado Springs. His stories have previously appeared in #34 ("Name the Planet"), #41 ("Milo Don't Count Coup") and #44 ("Milo on Fire"). His story in this issue is "Wild Seed".

**Stephen Palmer** is the author of seven published novels, including *Memory Seed* and *Glass* (Orbit), *Muezzinland,* and *Urbis Morpheos* (PS Publishing). His short fiction has been published by NewCon Press, Wildside Press, SF Spectrum, Rocket Science, Eibonvale Press, Unspoken Water, Infinity Plus and Solaris, plus two more currently unmentionable. Ebooks of all his novels have recently been published by Infinity Plus Ebooks, who will also be publishing his forthcoming novel *Hairy London.* He lives and works in Shropshire, UK. His story in this issue: "The Mines of Sorrow".

**Stephen Theaker** reviews all sorts of things in this issue. He even liked some of them. Further to last issue's editorial, he got up to 107 consecutive days of writing at least 250 words a day (getting up to an average of 837), before post-Nanowrimo fatigue kicked in and brought the run to a halt on December 5. His work has also appeared in *Black Static, Interzone, Prism,* the *BFS Journal,* and the letters page of the *NME.* (He wrote to defend the authenticity of the Manic Street Preachers, comparing them favourably with bands like Curve. Time has – as usual! – proven him quite right.)

# Black Ribbon

## Gary Budgen

Since the invasion of the city Isabel had worked with the black ribbon. Her office was in one of the old storage bunkers. Once, the whole complex would have offered a modicum of comfort: air conditioning, running water and overhead lighting. The storage room itself, sealed with perfect conditions for the black ribbon, was intact; but the rest of the complex had been reduced to little more than a set of holes or partially covered cellars connected by closed tunnels or trenches.

Isabel's office at least had a roof, but it was a dingy place, lit by a small electric lamp running from an extension cord hooked to the generator set up by the Captain and his men. She had a desk with a Bakelite telephone and a heavy manual typewriter. Also on the desk were the various machines on which she listened to the black ribbon. There was a clock on the wall but it had stopped. The hands had set at quarter to three, the time the invasion of the city had begun. Isabel had prised the hands off, not wanting to be reminded of her people's great shame. Now the clock was just a dial with Roman numerals. She found it oddly elegant.

The Captain had brought her here personally, seating her in the chair at the desk and looming over her from the other side. His uniform was entirely black except for some silver epaulettes and the piping around them. And of course the bright silver death's head badge on his cap.

"You will transcribe," he had said.

"Why?"

"The black ribbon must be transcribed."

"All of it?"

He had just shown her the storeroom, filled with black ribbon; some of it on large reels, other – more recent – in various formats of cartridges and cassettes.

"There is no time limit," he said, and he smiled for the first time, his white skin creasing around his mouth, his eyes still dull.

"And I expect," Isabel had said, "that there is more every day."

He turned away at that, facing through the walls of the bunker towards that part of the city where the conquest was not quite complete, where there was still some stubborn resistance.

"I have been to many places," he said. "Every city is different. In some places every moment of a person's life is inscribed in microdots on the retinas of their eyes. Other cities have people who live with crystals filled with hiero-glyphs inside their skulls. And here, here there is the black ribbon."

Yes, the Captain had been lots of places but he didn't seem to understand that the black ribbon was sacred, never to be listened to; only to be stored in the bunkers forever. The record of vanished lives.

"And what about you?" she'd asked, "How do you keep your life?"

The Captain had looked at her for a moment.

"We are the conquerors," he said, "We do not have to answer questions."

Isabel shrugged. She looked around the desk at the various machines. Some played reels and others played cassettes or cartridges.

"Very well," she said.

"The black ribbon must be transcribed," he said again, "All life must become text. You will listen to the black ribbon and transcribe. When you have finished your task the transcription will form a great chapter in the book we will send to God."

They fed her well enough and gave her cigarettes. Sometimes, to break the relentless misery of her work she would leave the office and go up to the surface. In the distance, across the rubble, she could see the flashes of fire and plumes of smoke from the other side of the city where the battles continued.

It was on such an occasion that she saw the resistance fighter try to kill the Captain. The fighter came out of the rubble somewhere and ran at the Captain with a knife. For a moment Isabel was filled with the thrill of the Captain's imminent demise. But the Captain pulled out his automatic pistol and shot the fighter, a young boy.

Isabel watched as the Captain crouched down and undid the boy's shirt. He opened the chest cavity and pulled out one of the new format micro-cassettes that had been used in recent years.

"Here," he said handing it to Isabel, "more black ribbon."

Then she went back down beneath the ground to her office.

She worked with no particular order, taking at random from the storeroom and playing the reels or cassettes or cartridges on the relevant machines and typing up as she listened.

It took about half a day to get through each life, an average life. Dead children were much quicker and once there was a ninety-year old woman who took from morning till long into the evening.

Isabel tried not to pause when she came across some particular highlight.

—*My tears when I held her in my arms after she had just been born, her hair so thin it was almost not there.*

—*As I walked into the apartment for the first time; after that riverside hovel it was so vast, like a cathedral.*

—*I know I am dying. I want to remember the verses they taught us at school.*

Many of the lives seemed, superficially, to be the same:

growing up; the first flush of love; the disappointments of middle age; the acceptance of aging. And yet each one had a rhythm of its own, or perhaps better to call it a flavour. Whatever it was she could not quite define it.

Isabel altered nothing, keeping the precise idioms and tense of the black ribbon recordings exactly. Some of the older reels had degraded, the magnetic particles worn away or the fixing agent so decrepit that the particles were simply no longer there at all. The lives on these old reels had become a series of fragments, odd words and phrases between white noise; but she transcribed these exactly as she heard them as well.

Then, one day, she found a black ribbon that was in a format she had not come across before. It was a large reel with a ribbon wider than would fit on any of the machines in her office. She thought of putting it aside but no; she would make the Captain work.

"I need a different machine for this," she told him, finding him on the surface looking through a pair of field-glasses.

He took the reel from her and weighed it in his hand.

"Very well," he said, "what do you require?"

"I will have to look."

He pondered this for a moment. Then he nodded.

He led her himself, through streets reduced to paths between ruins. They went through wrecked department stores where clothing hung on racks all covered with brick dust from shattered walls. She saw children's toys smashed into fragments of wood and plastic.

They found the right machine in an old radio repair shop and Isabel carried it as best she could. It was heavy and awkward and it was a long walk back to the bunker.

The attack came at dusk. Ragged resistance fighters, almost children, came at them. This time the Captain only managed to kill one before the other stuck a knife in his back.

"You're free," one of them said to Isabel.

She just stood there holding the tape machine.

"Come with us!"

"I can't," she said, "I must tend to the black ribbon."

They said nothing but nodded solemnly, recognising – as she now did – the sacred nature of her duty.

When they were gone she put down the tape machine and crouched next to the Captain. He was still alive.

"You must take it," he said.

"What?"

And he tapped his chest. She understood then that he too was from the city. That for him the invasion had been a homecoming.

"You are a traitor," she told him.

"We will all be in the book we will send to God," he said.

When he had gone she opened his chest cavity and took out a cassette in the standard format used until a decade or so ago. She pocketed this and picked up the machine and trudged back to the bunker.

In her office she set up the old machine salvaged from the radio repair shop. She placed the old reel on it and threaded the ribbon through the heads onto the counter reel. When she played it the sound was barely decipherable, mostly hiss and static interrupted by a few words she could make out here and there. She typed it all exactly as she heard it.

This then had been the fate of all those lives. Put into the bunker to preserve them into the future they would, instead, have degraded into incomprehensibility.

She placed the Captain's cassette on the desk and went up to the surface. It was night and she smoked a cigarette looking towards the other part of the city. It was oddly quiet; as though the war was at last over.

Soon she would go down to her office to transcribe another tape, to write another entry for the book that would be sent to God.

# Customs

## Mitchell Edgeworth

In the gulf between worlds is the vast desolation of space. The blackness, the void, a few molecules and atoms floating in emptiness. Pinpricks of starlight, like holes in a veil. But not truly empty. Between the planets and the asteroids, the stations and the clusters, are thousands upon thousands of spaceships, bearing the flags of every nation. Gargantuan grey freighters, pocked with micro-meteor craters and rusted with age, hauling gases and minerals downsystem. Sparkling cruise liners ferrying wealthy Martians to the pleasure rafts of Ganymede or the shining cities of Europa. Military frigates, ramshackle traders, private shuttles, Roma caravans, freelance explorers and prospectors. The radio waves crackle with a hundred different languages. So lonely, so desolate, yet even here humans have gone forth and multiplied.

See the *Black Swan*, bearing upsystem from Mars? See her solar collectors rotating slowly, the sun glinting on her cockpit, the fiery glow of her McEwan Mark IVs? Inside this cocoon of ageing alloys, through the thermal insulation and clusters of wiring and rats scurrying between her bulkheads, her crew are relieved and grateful to have escaped their bad turn of fortune on Mars. The pilot, Kingsford, is reading *Racing Review* on the flight deck with his feet up on the instrument panel. Chase, the first officer, is clouding the cramped space of the galley with steam as he shakes a wok of stir-fry. And the captain, Keiji – he drifts all over the ship, running his hands across the walls, feeling the throb of the engines, looking through the portholes at the motionless stars fixed against the ebony backdrop of the galaxy.

The *Black Swan* puts in at Novy Kratov, a former Russian prison rock with a grim population descended from those same dissidents and criminals. They stay here for two weeks, putting the final touches to the ship, welding and inspecting and re-working. A disagreement over the cost of parts leads to an altercation with a local mafia boss, and after some harsh words and gunshots the *Black Swan* escapes Novy Kratov under the same inauspicious circumstances as she fled Mars. Keiji is consumed by a foul mood, convinced that these departures are bad tidings. Kingsford reassures him they will find cargo at their next destination.

The *Black Swan* threads a path across the belt, visiting worlds all over the spectrum: from enormous cylinder cities to tiny waystations, from bioscaped pleasure resorts to former prison hellholes. Novy Kratov, Gallia, Halifax, New Barbuda, Outremer, St. Kaballa. Nowhere can they find cargo. Trading quotas are filled; harbourmasters shrug and apologise; private cargo has been monopolised by companies like Solar Express and ECS. As the *Black Swan* skips from asteroid to asteroid, Keiji watches his bank balance dwindle, and the feelings of exuberance and triumph he still clings to from their successful escape from Mars begin to fade.

After thirty-eight days threading her way across the asteroids, the *Black Swan* approaches Celestial Harbour, the greatest of the belt's trading hubs. The three of them watch it approach on the flight deck, Keiji and Chase with the awe of the uninitiated. A fifteen-kilometre asteroid, scooped out and spun to simulate gravity, so coated in radiation shielding and blast doors and telcom arrays that it no longer resembles a natural formation but rather a gigantic space station. A hundred docking struts, beaded with thousands upon thousands of spacecraft, from bulk ore carriers to private yachts. Titanic cargo robots crawling across the surface or clambering up and down the struts, unloading and offloading, machines and containers alike coated in garish high-visibility paint. Kingsford, who has been here hundreds of times, smiles at their fresh-faced amazement.

"This is the biggest city between Mars and Jupiter," he says. "Don't you worry. This is where we'll find our cargo. This is where it'll come together."

Keiji was feeling uneasy, which bothered him. He wasn't supposed to be feeling uneasy. He'd been feeling uneasy for years, tinkering with the ship in Elysium, patching and soldering and installing, wondering if he could ever really get it off the ground or if it was all the pipe dream of some spoilt rich idiot. Now he was finally here, in space, in a Chinese eatery in Celestial Harbour with the *Black Swan* safely docked on Strut 116, waiting for his crew to show up for dinner. Outside was the riotous clamour of a city of three million people, the streets crammed shoulder-to-shoulder with office blocks and skyscrapers and apartment buildings, every surface slick with advertising, the air clogged with antique engine fumes and the smell of ethnic cuisine and shouts in Mandarin. One of the system's greatest cities, crammed inside an eggshell asteroid hurtling around the sun. He was *here*! In an authentic foreign port, the registered captain of a proper goddamn spaceship! The dream had come *true*! So why was he feeling anxious, and vaguely depressed?

Keiji had spent the whole day trying to find cargo. While Chase had been sightseeing in Chengkou and Yang Plaza, and Kingsford had been catching up with various old friends and shady acquaintances, Keiji had been trawling along the dockyards and harbour offices in vain. It was just the same here as it had been in every one-horse asteroid they'd stopped off at since leaving Mars. Big or small, it made no difference – cargo was hard to come by. Most trade lines were tightly controlled by the big conglomerates, whether it was a shipping line transporting a five-thousand tonne cargo of helium-3 or a courier company delivering private packages. Tramp freighters like the *Black Swan* were increasingly uncommon, and most of them stayed afloat by smuggling: drugs, weapons, bioware, contraband and – inevitably – human beings. That was a world Keiji wanted no part in. And so, going over his bank records in this shitty yum cha restaurant in Celestial Harbour's industrial district, he found with a sinking sense of looming defeat that he'd already spent more than two thirds of what he considered to be the *Black Swan*'s "venture capital". Which was, really, his personal life savings.

He was startled out of his brooding as Chase sat down on the stool beside him. "This place is amazing," he grinned. The counter gave a view of the street outside, a wedge of concrete buttresses and grimy buildings crammed together above a brown canal. Electronics shops, news vendors, convenience stores and dive bars lined the pavement, and there was a steady bustle of workers in the evening rush hour – although Celestial Harbour had no day/night cycle, and there was nothing to differentiate this neon twilight from any other given hour of the day. It was a bleak and claustrophobic place, but Chase was genuine in his appreciation. He'd been far happier than usual since they'd left Mars behind; Keiji thought it might be the first time he'd seen him completely at ease ever since they'd met, and couldn't help but smile back at him. "Yeah. The Saturnians freak me out a bit, though."

"Probably good to get used to them before we ever go to Saturn."

"*If* we ever go there."

"Have you been looking for cargo?"

"Yes," Keiji said irritably. "What else do you think I'd be doing?"

Chase shrugged. "You ordered yet? I'm starving."

They slurped down noodles and dumplings as Keiji explained the day's failures to his first mate. Waiting for Kingsford, they tried some of the local beer, Tiandao, which tasted odd and gave Keiji a faint headache. Chase was on his fifth by the time the pilot showed up.

"Sorry I'm late," he said. "I was talking to an old buddy of mine at Strut 64. I might have some cargo for us."

Keiji perked up. "Really? What is it?"

Kingsford glanced around. The restaurant had largely emptied by this hour, and it was unlikely anyone there spoke English anyway, but he still lowered his voice. "Bioware. Unregistered. To a buyer on an asteroid called Cantabia. Right now it's about twelve days flying."

"No," Keiji said.

Chase opened his mouth, then hesitated. Kingsford glared at Keiji, and said "Why not?"

"I'm not fucking smuggling anything," Keiji said. "Are you out of your mind? They'd grab us before we even got through customs."

"No they wouldn't," Kingsford insisted. "You just wrap it all in flack paper and hide it in a bunch of legit stuff, like bananas."

"Bananas?"

"Or, I don't know, lumber! Whatever. It doesn't matter. You just hide it in genuine cargo. Customs here is a joke, I've done this a thousand times."

"Well, I don't know what your previous employers had their fingers in, but the *Black Swan* operates within the law," Keiji said frostily.

Kingsford rolled his eyes. "It's not like we were smuggling child sex slaves," he said. "It was just... stuff."

"What kind of stuff?" Keiji demanded.

"Bioware. Wire. Some guns, during the war."

"To which side?"

Kingsford snorted. "The Allies weren't exactly buying second-hand Chiangs from arms dealers."

Keiji's eyes slid over to Chase. "How do you feel about that?"

Chase shrugged. "They would have wound up there

sooner or later. War's a bit more complicated than that. Look, I think we should give this some thought."

Kingsford looked relieved; he'd forgotten Chase had been in the army, and thought he might have admitted to something grievously inappropriate. But his sour look returned when Keiji shook his head. "Oh, come on," he said. "How do you expect to stay aloft without doing this kind of thing? You got any *other* deals lined up?"

Keiji shook his head again. "Doesn't matter," he said. "I'm not going to lower myself to selling guns and drugs."

"We're not talking about guns and drugs!" Kingsford hissed. "We're talking about bioware. Medical nanytes. Physical enhancements. Nothing that's going to *hurt* anyone. And it wasn't *my* choice to start selling grenade launchers and sniper rifles to the rebels. I was just the pilot. So don't get all high and mighty with me!"

"Don't talk to your captain like that," Keiji glared.

"Guys..." Chase said.

"How do you expect to keep the ship running?" Kingsford shouted. "Money from your parents?"

"I paid for this ship myself! And if..."

Their argument was interrupted by the waiter, who shouted at them in broken English to take it outside. Keiji stood up and shoved the door open, the bell tinkling. Chase called after him but received no reply. He and Kingsford stood outside, the city's eternal night lit up by neon signs and vehicle headlights and the flare of street vendors' stoves.

"He'll cool off," Chase said reassuringly – but Kingsford was already stomping off in the other direction, embroiled in a huff of his own.

Chase sighed, and lit a cigarette. He suspected Keiji would come round to it eventually. If he didn't, the long dream of the *Black Swan* would abruptly disintegrate.

But he was off Mars again. That was the important thing. He never should have gone back in the first place. He took a long draught of the cigarette, and disappeared into foreign streets.

Over the next few days Keiji hunted all over the city for legitimate cargo. He trawled the bars and brothels of the harbour districts, spoke to warehouse suppliers and other freelance spacers, became lost in the tangles of lanes and side streets and alleyways. For lunch he retreated to Memorial Park, one of the few green spaces in the city, to buy a box of noodles from a vendor and sit on a bench watching the people go by.

More than anything else in Celestial Harbour – the skyscrapers dangling above him like stalactites, the engineers and civil workers drifting through the sky across the gravity spine, the sheer high density crush of it all – he found the people the most fascinating. Celestial Harbour was the conduit through which many travellers passed upsystem and downsystem, and it was swarming with people from hundreds of worlds: Ionese spacers, Hindu priests, Europan backpackers and Mercurian businessmen. Most intriguing of all were the Saturnians and free-state spacers, who adorned themselves with genetic modifications the way Westerners treated fashion: extra limbs, third eyes, chameleonic skin, spreading tufts of hair. Wings like dragons or angels or bats. Celestial Harbour had been founded more than a century ago as a Chinese resupply point en route to her Saturnian colonies, and while it had long ago become an independent city-state, it shared Saturn's laissez-faire attitude to genetic modification. New Tokyo, Lucia and most of the other asteroid trading hubs were firm signatories to the Watson-Crick Treaty, and wouldn't permit genetically-modified spacers to leave their harbour zones. Keiji, who had been given a conservative Martian education, found it horrifying and disgusting to see human beings debase themselves in such a way – but at the same time it was amazing and a little exciting. This was why he was here. To be amongst these people. To see these places.

At the centre of the park, surrounded by flower gardens and koi ponds, was a memorial to the 72-hour War and the lost Earth. Below a statue of huddled refugees, a creed was spelled out in Mandarin and English:

IN GRIEVING FOR OUR LOST HOME
AND WITH GRATITUDE FOR OUR NEW
WE WILL REMEMBER THEM

Keiji unclipped his watch and ran his hands over its joints and buckles. It was earthware; his great-grandfather had bought it in Amsterdam the day before he flew to Kenya, went up the space elevator and travelled to Mars to work in the mines. Only a few short months later, the war broke out, and he had found that Mars would be his home forever. The watch had been passed down from father to son. Keiji's own father had given it to him the day he left home for university. Later, when things had changed, he had demanded it back. Keiji had refused.

He couldn't go back to Mars. He had to keep the *Black Swan* in the sky.

When Keiji returned to the *Black Swan*, in her docking port at the end of Strut 116 high above the outer shell of the asteroid, he found Kingsford and Chase in quiet discussion in the mess. They looked up at him guiltily as he entered. "Talking about me?" Keiji asked.

"We need to take this cargo," Kingsford said quietly. "You've been looking for five days now. You've found nothing. You're not..."

"I know," Keiji said wearily, sinking onto the couch and pulling his boots off. "We're going to take it."

"We can't..." Kingsford said, then blinked in surprise and said "What? Really?"

"Yes. Call your friend. Organise it. We'll take it."

"Okay. Great. Great!" He stood up and hurried off towards the airlock.

Keiji sank down into the couch and closed his eyes. "What changed your mind?" Chase asked.

"I don't know. I don't want to do it. This is the thin end of the wedge." Keiji opened his eyes suddenly and looked him in the face. "I can do this once and say that's it. You know? But it will make it easier to do it again, and again, and pretty soon we'll be smuggling drugs and guns and we won't think it's any big deal. All those captains out there who do that kind of thing... you think they just don't care? Some of them, sure. But I bet a lot of them had consciences at first. And they squashed down on them. Because they 'had' to do it. For money. And before long..." He waved an arm.

"You don't have to do anything you don't want to," Chase said.

Keiji snorted. "I wouldn't have thought so either, but here we are. My first mate is on the run from both the police and the Mangala Tong. My pilot I had to rescue from armed gangsters, which ended up in a public shootout in Elysium City. And I... well, now I'm smuggling illegal bioware from Celestial Harbour to some asteroid I've never even heard of. I can picture myself describing all this in court one day."

"If it's any consolation," Chase said, "I didn't think my life would turn out like this either."

Keiji snorted again. "Yeah, I know *your* story."

Chase narrowed his eyes. "What? You're better than me now?"

"You made your decisions."

Chase was startled, and suddenly angry. "What? I made the decision to do the right thing! I sacrificed *everything* I had! To protect people! And you... you think you've got it hard because the world isn't making everything easy for you on your rich-kid spaceship lark?" He rounded on the captain with a venomous fury, something Keiji had never seen before. "Apologise! Fucking apologise!"

For a moment Keiji thought Chase was about to hit him,

and shrunk back into the couch in alarm, his hand raised. "Okay! Jesus! Sorry... yeah, I am, I am, I'm sorry. It's not the same thing. I know. It's just... I don't want to do this. You understand that, don't you? Isn't this the kind of thing you used to try to *stop* from happening?"

His first mate relented, backing away, the fury draining from his face. It was replaced with something Keiji couldn't read. "Yeah," he said. "Used to." Then he left.

Keiji struggled to his feet and went to peer out of one of the portholes. He could see the long gantry of the docking strut, dropping vertiginously down to Celestial Harbour. Engineers in suits crawling over the hull of a private transport, soldering and repairing; robots loading cargo into a bulk carrier; tiny sightseeing pods floating about the place, pointing out the wonders of the exterior harbour web to tourists. Far below was the armoured, dust-frosted bulk of the asteroid itself, containing that fragile blip of human existence, a stifling city of three million people, hurtling itself through the emptiness of space.

He couldn't go back.

Kingsford's associates arrived the next day, with cargo robots bearing six large pallets of vacuum crates. The strut's customs officials ran over them with x-rays and sensors, and opened one up to rifle around in it. Keiji's heart was thrumming as he watched, trying to keep a straight face. "Machinery parts, special order," one of the deliverymen said in Mandarin. The bored officer nodded and waved them through. Keiji signed and fingerprinted the customs forms while they deposited them in the hold of the *Black Swan*.

"See?" Kingsford grinned as they closed the cargo doors. "Nothing to it." But the captain was already clomping up the stairs, disappearing into his cabin.

The twelve day voyage to Cantabia was an awkward one. Keiji spent most of it shut up in the captain's quarters, sulking and brooding. Less than two months off Mars and already the atmosphere had soured. "When's he going to get over this?" Kingsford asked Chase one morning, when he brought the pilot a mug of coffee on the flight deck.

"I dunno. Maybe after we finish this trade and we get the money."

"I don't know why he's so goddamn finicky about it," Kingsford muttered. "You'd think we were selling wire to orphans."

"Why *is* bioware trading illegal, anyway?"

"Because the companies want it to be directly implanted in one of their own medicos," Kingsford said. "Partly to try to stamp out reverse-engineering, and partly so they get the trade, and partly because that way they can oversee it and make sure people are getting legit products. The bioware we have in the hold right now is counterfeit, no question."

"Well, then he has a point. If we're just delivering second-rate stuff..."

"They *know* it's second-rate stuff. It's still better than nothing. It's easy for us. If you're born on Mars, you're constitutionally guaranteed to be given medical bioware. It's a birthright. Same for Europa and Ganymede and Mercury and all the other rich worlds. But just you wait till you see some of the places out in the belt. Living standards are pretty crap out here. The infrastructure, the safety standards... well, just wait and see. I've been from one end of this system to the other, and believe you me, there are places out there that will make you drop to your knees and praise God that you were born on Mars."

Chase tried sparking up a conversation with Keiji when he emerged from his room, to take a shower or get food from the galley, but he was met with nothing but grunts and monotone responses. Eventually he was consumed by his own bitter anger. Why did he have to be so difficult? What if it made the whole venture fall apart? Chase was growing comfortable on the *Black Swan*, now that it was off Mars.

He'd never entirely been at ease when it was in the junkyard in Elysium; his cabin had been mostly bare and his clothes still in his army rucksack, ready to flee at a moment's notice. Now he was beginning to unpack, leave his things lying around, personalise his space with trinkets and souvenirs he'd picked up in various ports. He was growing to like Kingsford, despite his gruff nature, and Keiji was the closest friend he'd had in years. Even with the low-key anxiety that would forever curse him on his homeworld, he'd been a damn sight happier in the junkyard than he had been for years before that.

And now it might all fall apart, because Keiji was too much of an uptight control freak. Because he refused to bend the rules.

Eventually Chase grew tired of it all, and knocked on the captain's door. He entered the room to find Keiji sitting on his bed, scrolling through text files. "What are you reading?"

"My old journals," Keiji said. "What do you want?"

"I want you to come out of your cabin and talk to us," Chase said. "I want you to stop being so fucking difficult about this. Why does it matter so much?"

"Because this wasn't how it was supposed to be," Keiji said. "This wasn't what I thought we'd be doing."

"So why are we doing it, then? Jettison the fucking stuff if you feel like that! This is the most we've spoken in a week. You can't just sit in here all day."

Keiji said nothing.

"What are you going to do when we get to Cantabia?" Chase asked.

"I don't know. Sell this shit, I guess. Sell it to some mob boss or corrupt governor or whoever it is Kingsford has arranged for us. Let them hock it off to people who think it's genuine Rubicon. And then take off with the money, so we're not there to see it in a few years when they malfunction and people's blood vessels start bursting or cancers sprout up all over them."

It sounded like a rehearsed speech to Chase, and he tried

not to roll his eyes. "We don't have to sell it," he said. "If that's how you feel, we can jettison it. Forget about it, and move on."

"I have too much money tied up in it," Keiji said. "And anyway, what do we do then? We're back where we started. No trade, no prospects, no hope." He looked up at Chase. "It's pretty simple. I can either start doing shit like this, or I can sell the ship and go crawling back to Zutphen."

Chase didn't know what to say. After a moment, he left the room, leaving Keiji in the glow of his computer screen, reading the hopes and dreams of a vanished man.

Twelve days out of Celestial Harbour the homing beacon of Cantabia began pinging on their navigation screens. Before long, the asteroid itself blossomed into view, a grey potato with a few blast doors and radar domes sprouting from its surface. Keiji begrudgingly slunk up onto the flight deck to watch it approach, and Kingsford pulled its profile up on the main screen.

"Portuguese-speaking," he said. "A Brazilian prison and mining colony, founded 2085. Abandoned after the war, left to its own devices, limped along for a while on mining exports before they all dried up. Population 8,000, and dropping."

"Why isn't it spinning?" Chase asked.

Kingsford shrugged. "It's not spun. Most of the prison colonies weren't, until people tried to pretty them up into proper worlds. Places like Cantabia just never had the money for it."

"So they're just living in zero gravity?"

"Yup. Now shut up, I gotta concentrate for the approach."

Kingsford brought the *Black Swan* in on a steady curve, swinging her around to the leeward side of the asteroid, where a docking bay opened up to accept them. The radio crackled with instructions in Portuguese, which the ship's computer translated for them. "Might want to suit up," Kingsford said. "And grab mine for me."

"What? Why?"

"You didn't catch that? Their harbour's not properly pressurised. Too dangerous to go walking around in the open."

Keiji and Chase went down to the cargo bay to fetch the ship's spacesuits, which they'd bought at an Army surplus store in Aaru. "This is so fucked," Keiji muttered. "What kind of a place is this?"

They felt the *Swan* heave and groan as Kingsford brought her into the docking clamps, and as the engines cut out and the artificial gravity ceased, they felt the sudden, stomach-lurching dizziness of zero gravity. They pulled on their clinging, rubbery suits and helmets and stared out the portholes as Kingsford came down the stairwell and struggled into his own.

The spaceport – if it could be called that – had seen better days. It was only large enough to hold a few small freighters or shuttles, and the docking clamps in the other bays looked rusted shut. A collection of random crates and boxes were scattered about. Half the lights had burst and the other half were flickering, and the safety gauges above the airlocks were flashing red warning signs in Portuguese. "Seriously fucked," Keiji muttered.

After a few moments one of the interior airlocks opened, and a group of figures in spacesuits of eclectic design floated into the bay. Using rungs clumsily welded onto the steel floor, they quickly made their way over to the *Black Swan* and waited expectantly around the cargo hatch. Chase shrugged, and hit the controls. The cargo bay doors slowly rose open, and the three of them drifted out to meet the landing party.

"Captain DuVal, I presume?" one of the men said over his suit comms, reaching forward to encase Keiji's hand in a rubbery grip.

"Yeah."

"Pleasure to meet you. Carlos Vanzolina, governor and harbourmaster of Cantabia. Welcome to our home." His

English was superb, but delivered in an almost risible Latin accent.

"It's... nice to be here," Keiji said.

"Thank you. My men will verify your cargo, with your permission?"

Keiji shrugged. "Sure."

"Excellent. It will take some time; there is no need for us to stay here. Please, come join me in my office."

The three of them followed Vanzolina outside while his men began unpacking the crates. They pushed off from the floor and drifted up towards a catwalk, where an airlock led into a spacious office. Like everything else on Cantabia, it was decaying, but it was a relief to remove their helmets, even if the air smelled stale and fetid.

A broad window on one side of the office surveyed the landing bay; a window on the other side looked over a long, dark street, stretching through the heart of the asteroid. Cantabia seemed little changed from the days when it had been a prison colony. It was not a city street, full of bustle and life, like Celestial Harbour or Halifax or even Novy Kratov. It was more of a service corridor, stretching between gloomy ranks of steel and concrete dwellings. A few figures were floating up and down the street, wearing spacesuits, often with ill-fitting helmets and different coloured gloves. Some of them looked fifty years out of date.

"You have no atmosphere," Keiji said in dismay.

"Oh, yes," Vanzolina said, rummaging in his drinks cabinet, "but a tenuous one. We had a breach last month, so I've given a general order for suits to be worn in public spaces. The inner buildings are still sound. Well, most of them. We have a shipment of replacement seals due in from Mars next month." He found a few mismatched glasses with zero-g lids, and poured them each a shot of whiskey before raising his in a toast. "To commerce!" he smiled, and downed his glass in one suck.

Keiji smiled uncertainly, and drank his own. There was something profoundly sad about having to serve a guest whiskey in a sippy cup. "So what's the bioware for?" he asked.

"The children, mostly," Vanzolina said, drifting over from the table to join him by the window. "Zero gravity does terrible things to the human body, you know? It has cumulative effects over the generations. Curved spines, warped bones, weak muscles. Not to mention the radiation shielding. It's been getting worse over last twenty, thirty years. Cancer rates, more than eighty per cent."

"Oh my god," Keiji murmured. "Why... well, no offence, but... why do you *live* here?"

Vanzolina looked at him with a mixture of pity and disbelief. "Who would take us?"

*Eight thousand people*, Keiji thought. How many more, crammed into the thousands of barely liveable asteroids scattered in a vast ring around the sun?

Keiji had always known he was privileged. But he'd always compared his privilege to other Martians, compared his canalside mansion in Zutphen to their two-bedroom flats, compared his Reeve scholarship to their dead-end jobs. He'd never realised the privileges that even the lowest of Martian citizens enjoyed – the sky, the air, the trees.

He'd spent three years fixing the *Black Swan* up and dreaming of taking her out into the system without ever thinking of what the system would be like. He'd never stopped to think that, for so many people, the destruction of Earth – something that was, to a Martian, no more than a chapter in the history books – had continuing, devastating repercussions for almost half the human race.

"There are places worse off than we are," Vanzolina said. "Asteroids that cannot even grow their own food, where people are starving to death. Starvation, in this century! The larger worlds have refugee quotas; they will only absorb so many people per year. And they prefer for us to stay here – to bring our worlds up to a bare minimum of living standards. We had some engineers and technicians from

Ganymede here ten years ago. They fixed a few things, repaired our comms, gave us new raw supply for the food vats. But it all comes apart again. It's just too old. What we need is a complete refit. Not a bioscaping, just an overhaul. But who knows how much that would cost?"

Keiji thought of New Barbuda, an asteroid they'd visited shortly before Celestial Harbour. A bioscaped world designed to resemble the tropical islands of Old Earth, with powder-white sand and coconut trees and Martian and Europan tourists lazing on the beach. Jet skis and barbecues and easy living. It cost no more to maintain a bioscaped asteroid like New Barbuda than it did to maintain a rust-bucket like Novy Kratov. It was just the initial costs that were mindblowing. And with the Humanity Project having petered out...

"That's why I'm buying from good men like yourself," Vanzolina continued. Keiji was starting to feel bad about finding his accent amusing. "Engine parts, bioware, medicine, food... many asteroids resort to piracy. We aren't at that point yet. God willing, during my life, we never will be."

Vanzolina's radio crackled in Portuguese, and he glanced out the harbour window. His men had finished verifying and unloading the cargo, and gave him the thumbs up from down below. He turned and shook Keiji's hand again, grasping his forearm. "Once again, captain, we truly appreciate your effort. I understand how risky it is to smuggle bioware out of a place like Celestial Harbour. I cannot thank you enough for this."

Keiji hesitated. "It wasn't that hard. It was for the money."

"Of course. But still. You have done a good thing, captain. Would you care to stay with us, this evening?"

"Oh... I'm afraid not, no. We have a schedule to keep. We're headed for Lucia."

Vanzolina nodded in assent. "I understand. Do you need food, or water? Oxygen?"

"No, we're fully loaded. Thank you, though."

"Not at all. We can't thank you enough! There are children

here, now, who will have a chance. You will always be welcome here. Safe travels, captain."

They farewelled the governor, and drifted back down the loading bay towards the *Black Swan*. Chase and Kingsford stared at Keiji the entire time. Eventually, as they waited for the ship's airlock cycle to finish, he could no longer avoid their eyes.

"Oh, *all right*," he admitted.

# The Lazarus Loophole

## Josie Gowler

"So who do we have today?" I ask.

Dave rattles through the delivery note from Upstairs. "Two wanting-to-stay-rich divorcees, one deposed dictator, a murderer – allegedly – and that terrorist guy who was on the news last week."

"Nice," I mutter, scratching my beard. "Rack 'em up."

We get to work. Folks think it's just about lobbing them in a freezer, but there is some skill involved. The sensors go on, then we attach them to the extracorporeal membrane oxygenation machines – oxys for short – and do the computer hook-ups. Then we chill them right down. All within ten minutes of death.

The silence and the focus end when the last dead dude is plugged in and put in cold store. Dave and I look at each other across the terrorist's corpse and share a smile. There's always that frisson of concern that something will go wrong, that someone who's paid more money than I can even dream of to get this done to them will actually die on us. Properly die, I mean. Not the temporary wipe-the-slate-clean stuff we have here.

"Right, death certificates next, then lunch, then we can start shoving oxygen back into batch 3225 and waking 'em up."

"All shiny and new and not guilty any more," Dave replies. He pauses. "Julian?"

"Yeah?" I'm already starting on the first certificate of today's batch.

"Does it bother you?"

I roll my eyes. Not this again. "Do you think I'd work here if it did?" I hate it when Dave gets all philosophical but I guess arguing with him helps me to look convincing. And I've thought of a new tack today. "Look, in any society, you'll always find someone willing to be a hangman. Doesn't mean they're a bad person. This is the same, but flipped on its head. The hangman doesn't care if the person they're dispatching is guilty or not, and neither do we. Now quit the debate. *Please*."

"And we're making a load of money while we do it."

"Uh-huh." Desperate to avoid another round of discussion, I head Dave off while he's still forming more words. "Look, why don't you grab us lunch while I finish up the paperwork? It'll save time later."

He nods and after a few pleasantries of the sushi-or-sandwich variety, he wanders off.

I pause for a few seconds, in case he's forgotten his wallet again. Once I'm sure that he's gone, I jump up from my chair.

I start pulling the plugs. The whirr of machinery decreases in increments. I pause at the terrorist. I can't even bring myself to whisper his name. I rub the scars just under my collar. I've been dreaming of this moment, waiting undercover for a year. Now I want to say something to his inert body, but the words won't come. I unplug the machine and smile. These bastards may have counted on the ultimate legal loophole here on Proximo Two, but they hadn't counted on me. Yes, crimes get extinguished a year and a day after death, as do marriages. So I'm the mop-up. And I'm damned glad to be doing it.

I leave the divorcees. I don't know enough about them or their wives to make an informed decision. Good luck to 'em. Three minutes later I'm out of the revolving doors of the clinic and on my way to the spaceport. Back to Proximo Three's counter-terrorism unit, back to my old life. Ready to swap notes with the others. Ready for the next assignment. Hangman or assassin? It doesn't matter to me.

# The Mines of Sorrow

## Stephen Palmer

"This is the suit of armour that you will be required to wear now you are taking over your father's position."

Gravis studied the object indicated by the Secretary of the Sorrow Guild. "And my father wore this all the time?" he said.

"Yes, sir. You will be required to wear it also."

"*All* the time?"

"You are your father's eldest son," said the Secretary, "and responsibility for leading the Sorrow Guild falls upon your young shoulders. I am certain, sir, that you will accept that responsibility."

Gravis shook his head. Still stunned by the news of his father's death, he glanced at the old man standing beside him: the Secretary, calm and assured. "I suppose I must," he murmured.

"There is no suppose about it, sir. You must."

Gravis approached the suit of armour, which hung from an oblong frame suspended from the ceiling of the Sorrow Guild's family study. The room was dense with the paraphernalia of his father: that desk, those stuffed foxes, the box of cigars, that row of umbrellas standing beneath the hat stand. The smell of old smoke and his father's brand of hair oil.

The suit of armour shone like glass before a sunset. The main window lay a few yards away, a low sun shining through it; the armour radiated orange light as if channelling heavenly fire from some distant, spectral region. "Is it made of glass?" he asked.

"Nobody knows, sir."

"But if my father wore it all the time, why didn't he glow? Why didn't we notice him wearing it?"

"Put it on sir, and you will find out the answers to those questions."

Gravis shrugged. "Do I have to do it now?"

"If you do not, the security of the Sorrow Guild will remain uncertain. You would not want that, would you?"

"Er... no."

Gravis approached the suit of armour until he stood just a foot away. He narrowed his eyes so that the orange glow was all he could see, shimmering and sparkling.

"How do I put it on?" he asked.

"Like any other garment, sir. Over your head."

Gravis took hold of the suit of armour. It felt like warm cloth. It was not made of glass, it was almost like a person beneath his hands, a thing of living flesh. Then it came loose from the frame and dropped; and he caught it, then raised it over his head and let it slip over him.

"There you are, sir. That was not so difficult, was it?"

"I feel different." Gravis looked down at himself. He appeared the same. The armour was invisible, though he could feel it against his clothes like the finest, lightest undergarment of silk. "What's happened to me?"

"You are the Guildmaster of the Sorrow Guild, sir," the Secretary replied. "Of course you feel different. That armour protects you against the blows and random tragedies of life, as well as against the weapons of the enemy. You will find yourself becoming more like your father in temperament, as you retire from your old life and take up the burdens of the Sorrow Guild. I am confident that you will be as proficient, and perhaps even as wise as your remarkable forebear."

"How do I take it off when I go to bed, or have a bath?"

"You never take it off, sir."

Gravis took a deep breath. "Thank you, er... er... I don't think I was ever told your name."

"I do not have a name, sir. I am the Secretary of the Sorrow Guild."

"You don't have a name?"

"So I am told, sir. Would you like a glass of wine now?"

The graveyard of Sorgian town lay at the edge of the settlement, with the shadow of Zorg Ridge a cloud-topped, dark brown mass five miles away. Yet despite that distance, the ridge – two thousand feet high and clothed in moorland vegetation – was the most prominent aspect of the graveyard, for beneath those desolate hills sorrow was mined.

Grever glanced at his brother. The funeral had not gone as he had expected. His mother wept, his cousins wept, *he* wept, but his brother was cool and calm; emotionless, almost. And Grever did not know why: and Grever did not like this new brother.

The Secretary of the Sorrow Guild conducted the service, reading from ancient books kept over endless millennia in secret vaults. His position too was hereditary, his son, just ten, at his side, whey-faced and trembling with nerves.

Grever whispered to Gravis, "What's the matter?"

Gravis glanced at him, before the slightest of frowns appeared on his face. "What do you mean?"

"Aren't you upset?"

"It is my father who's gone."

"Yes, but aren't you *upset?*"

Gravis looked away, as if the question was too unimportant for him to bother with.

Grever felt insulted. He thought well of his brother and they had a reasonable relationship, but this mask of rectitude was unlike him. Why wasn't he crying? He said, "Look at mother, she's wept a raincloud. What's wrong with you?"

"Stop asking me questions."

Grever began to fidget. "What happened in father's study? Did you eat something that's made you stiff as a plank? It's *dad* who's died."

"I know who has died, Grever. Why are you telling me the obvious?"

"Because you're not –"

"*Shhh!*"

The Secretary had paused his sermon and was staring in Grever's direction. Red-faced, Grever looked down at his shoes.

The sermon continued.

"Water becomes water, ashes become ashes, and we stand here in the knowledge of the surety of butterflies ascending into the skies, to be lost amongst the eternal clouds..."

Grever whispered, "Are you the Guildmaster already?"

"Will you stop asking me stupid questions?"

"Oh, now they're stupid are they? My goodness, the moment you get your hands on the steering wheel you think you're the greatest person in Sorgian –"

"Shut up, you little fool. I *am* the most important person in Sorgian, but it's not my fault. I didn't ask to be born, did I? I happened to be the eldest son, and now you are annoyed that nobody is paying you any attention."

Grever hissed, "Lies! You trot out that excuse *every* time, just because you think you're more important than me –"

"Shhh! Mother's staring at you. She wants you to have some respect for the dead, and for the Secretary too – he is giving our own father the last rites, don't you understand? Now be quiet and do as I've told you."

Grever clamped down on his anger, staring once again at his shoes. He had never been spoken to like this by his own brother. Fractured memories of his past flashed before his mind's eye: playing with toys, Gravis on the trucks and he on the trains; his mother making them damson stew and cream; his father patting him on the head...

He felt tears trickling down his cheeks once again. He glanced at Gravis: face of stone, gaze distant, body unmoving.

"You're a machine, Gravis. They ought to put you in –"

"Will you be quiet?"

All at once Grever's self-control broke. He turned on Gravis and yelled, "No, *you* listen to me! *You're* the one disrespecting our dad, because *you're* the one just standing there like a statue! What's the matter, don't you know you're at a funeral?"

He tottered away from the crowd towards the open grave.

"Oh, dad, I don't want you to go! It's too early. Why did you have to go just *now?*"

And the Secretary looked at him as though he was an autumn leaf fluttering in the breeze.

Grever shouted at him, "And *you* can shut up too, you useless, dry old piece of paper! I *hate* you! What have you done to my family, eh?"

There came no reply. Sobbing, Grever ran out of the graveyard, turning to face Zorg Ridge. Moaning to himself he ran on, and his tears fell on the dry and dusty road to leave a trail of dark spots for all to see.

The guns of the Happiness Guild were multi-barrelled, set on rotating mounts that an operator, sitting in the jockey-chair hung from the rear of the weapon, could move with a flick of the wrist. They were massive devices, black and wreathed in smoke, but their inertia was low, and those thick, heavily muscled mounts were well greased.

Gaudere peered through the long range viewfinder at the road leading up to the Mines of Sorrow. She was not sure, but...

Could it be him? Her heart leaped. She loved just to look at him, at his handsome face, his dark, floppy-fringed hair, at his athletic body. She touched a control and swung the gunsight around so that she could get a better look. Yes, it was him; it was Grever.

She bit her lower lip. She was *so* sweet on him. But he was a man of the opposite guild.

Was it the danger? Was it just physical? She did not know, or care. There was some kind of elemental attraction between them, she knew it and so did he.

Again she peered at Grever through the gunsight as he ran towards the mine workings. He seemed to be heading straight for the openings – nine black holes set in a line along the lower bank of Zorg Ridge – but surely he must stop soon. Nobody could enter the Mines of Sorrow without protective clothing; too intense for an unarmoured human mind to cope with.

But he was not slowing down. Her heartbeat began to race, and there came a dull thudding to her ears. Grever! She could not lose him, even though their love was hopeless.

Rule number one of the Happiness Guild: never fire your gun at a person. She thumbed the power down to minimum and set the crosshairs to follow Grever. The weapon thrummed, its joyous vibrations passing into her body through the webbing of the chair in which she was suspended. Her legs felt warm; too warm.

She touched the button and fired the gun. A stream of supersonic white butterflies burst from the nozzle and sped towards Grever, the subtle sound of their motion like the crack of a feather whip. There came a burst of perfume as the smoke cleared. Gaudere peered through the gunsight to see Grever writhing on the ground.

That did not look good...

She wiped the report of what she had done from the gun's inventory.

That also was forbidden. But she would do anything for Grever.

Grever peered at the nearest mine working, the entrance to which lay just fifty feet away. With his body in spasm he was unable to walk: his vision destroyed by whiteness, hissing in his ears, his nose filled with too-sweet perfume.

But he hung on to consciousness. The dank smell of sorrow moved like a trickle of mud through a pool of water, and he clung on to it with all the intensity of his grief-empowered mind. He crawled through the butterfly debris, he rejected their charms, he ignored their siren song, fixing his mind with total concentration on the thin rope that promised cool safety, dark safety, underground. And as he crawled nearer, though his body was aflame with joy, he felt his grief return, strengthen, as if conducted like electricity through the cable of sadness that snaked out to him from subterranea.

Then the mine entrance appeared and his vision cleared. The joy was fading. If he had not just lost his father he would be a dead man for sure, but the raw surge of grief in his mind had saved him from the enemy.

Then everything went dark.

He was underground. He turned, to see a circle of blue sky beside him, that he knew he had just crawled through. He was safe...

But now he did not know what to do. The dangers were close, present, obvious: an unprotected man in the Mines of Sorrow. He could be consumed by grief here, could become suicidal. But he did not care. The shock of his father's death, the stark reality of the funeral, the horror of his brother's emotionless face... oh, what was the point of anything? He might as well give up now and surrender to the power of the stuff they mined here.

He walked into the mines, uncaring.

Time passed unmarked. He heard the distant rumble of the machines used by the miners of the Sorrow Guild to extract that intense, black substance so precious to this land, which had given Sorgian its wealth and the Sorrow Guild its power. He smelled it, saw it alight on the bare skin of his arms like soot from a chimney. The blackness of grief.

And then a voice.

"What are you *doing* here, mate? You're not wearing any gear!"

Grever looked up. The light from a lantern held by a nearby figure momentarily dazzled him. The figure was a humanoid blob, entirely covered in thick canvas stained black by raw sorrow, that stank in Grever's nostrils like burnt hair. Two arms, two legs and a head; a big black amoeba. Then the figure wiped sorrow off the glass front of the helmet like grease off a plate, and his face was revealed, pale, eyes staring: a man. A miner.

"Get out of here, you fool!" the miner cried.

Grever shook his head. "No, I don't want to."

"But... how have you managed to get this far without protective clothing?"

It was a good question. Grever considered it, intrigued despite himself. "I don't know," he said. "I should be dead by now."

Then the man stared, and raised one blob of an arm to point. "There's something white on your shoulder." He gasped, then groaned. "*Contamination!*"

Gravis sat at the study desk and pondered the fact that it was now his. This desk, this repository of all things fatherly, was now *his*. He, in a sense, was his father. But he was inexperienced, unmarried. He needed an heir now. He would have to find a woman; any woman would do. But he was not good with women.

The Secretary knocked on the study door, then entered the room. "Sir, there has been an incident in the mines."

Gravis sat up, leaned forward and steepled his hands, resting his elbows on the leather-clad surface of the desk. "An incident?"

The Secretary nodded, then approached. "Somebody has got into the mines, somebody unauthorised. He did not wear protective garb. And our agents atop Zorg Ridge are reporting an anomalous burst of happiness."

"Really?"

The Secretary nodded. "What are your orders, sir?"

Gravis stood up. "We will have no happiness at our mines. The enemy plan tricks to destabilise our guild." He took a cigar from the box on the desk and lit it. Puffing to intensify the burning, he said through the side of his mouth, "I shall go there myself. Power up the truck. Fill its tank with fuel. We head out of Sorgian for the hills."

In Grever's pocket there lay an old cigarette case that he had stolen years ago from his father's bedroom. Hands in pockets, hardly daring to glance down at the white shape on his shoulder, he felt that case, though for a moment did not recognise what it was. Then he grasped it, withdrew it and opened it. The miner nodded, his eyes wide and staring behind the sorrow-smeared visor of his helmet.

Grever held the case upside-down, then brought it down over the butterfly.

He relaxed, and the miner sagged inside his suit, as if exhausted. Contamination was a miner's worst fear: a particle meets an anti-particle...

"Who are you?" the miner asked.

Grever had to think for a moment. The strength of the emotion he had felt and the shocks of the day had all conspired to put him into what seemed a parallel state of mind, where he just acted on impulse, not caring if he lived or died, if he hurt somebody or withdrew from the world. Not even caring about his family and his friends.

At length he cleared his throat and said, "I'm Grever –"

"Grever? The son –"

"Yes! Yes... but he's gone now."

"Of course, of course..." The miner seemed embarrassed, though it was difficult to tell through all that canvas clothing. "I think we'll take you up to the pit, young Grever. You need some fresh air and something to protect you. There's clothes up there."

Grever shrugged. "All right. But I don't care."

"Well you *should*."

Grever shrugged again. The miner took him by the hand, but Grever jerked his arm back as the sheen of sorrow on the man's protectives burst like a muddy fountain over his sensorium; for a second he had felt as though he was drowning.

"Sorry," said the miner. "Force of habit. Follow me, and quickly. I still don't understand why you're alive."

"Nothing here to kill myself with –"

"That's *enough* of that kind of talk, young man."

They trudged through the mine tunnel, taking every shaft that led upwards until they arrived at the pit, where Grever saw blue sky and smelled a hint of damp heathland. This was the original mine working – open cast – created centuries ago by the inhabitants of Zorg Ridge, which then, in warmer times, was a pleasant place to live. He saw a number of sheds built around the puddle-splashed perimeter of the pit, one of which the miner approached. A few moments later the miner entered one of the sheds then reappeared carrying a black bag.

He threw it at Grever's feet and said, "Put that on. It'll protect you against the worst of the stuff. Though your skin's absorbing it even as I speak. I think that butterfly saved you."

Grever pulled out the cigarette case and put it on the floor, then dressed in the protective gear. He began to feel better almost at once, as if a fog was rolling back from his mind. His eyes felt wide, open; not tired any more. The sense of fatigue that tugged at his muscles faded. He began to remember things. He remembered Gaudere.

"I want to get out now," he said.

"You'll be rescued soon enough. There's an alarm button in that shed. Your brother'll get the call, or more likely the Secretary will."

Grever nodded. He opened the cigarette case and let the butterfly flap out. It ascended into the sky, white against blue, until it was lost amidst the roiling vapour of a rain-cloud.

"Gone," he said.

The miner nodded. "Could have blown the place up."

"Why didn't it?"

"I think you've had a couple of bad days Grever, if you don't mind me saying so. It was trapped on you, weighed down by your grief."

"A black slug will eat it. Or the other way round."

The miner shook his head. "Butterflies don't eat slugs.

You ever wonder why that was, or did your father maybe tell you?"

Grever frowned. "No. "

"Because happiness comes from within, but grief comes from the world around. You should think about that. You see, Grever, a lot of us miners don't think you're in the right guild."

Grever took a few paces away from the miner. He was getting cold, now.

Gaudere noticed the Happiness Guild marshal when she was only a hundred yards away and it was too late to run. She checked that she had wiped the report of the butterfly firing from the gun's inventory.

The marshal, a middle aged woman wearing white leather garments and boots, approached and without saying a word disabled the firing catch.

"What are you doing?" Gaudere asked. "I'm on duty."

"We had a report of an unethical firing."

Gaudere shrugged. "Check the inventory, there's nothing there."

The marshal ran a report from the gun's records, then grimaced. "I know what you did."

"You might think you know, but you need proof... oh!"

A dark, slimy shape crawled over the marshal's shoulder, a shape six inches long with two eyes on stalks. Gaudere, her face pulled into a rictus of disgust, jumped off the jockey-chair and stumbled away. Already the marshal was on the ground, her face in the mud. Then a hand grabbed Gaudere.

She span around to see a tall man with cropped hair and a dark grey uniform staring at her. His face was familiar.

"You," he said, "will be accompanying me to the Mines of Sorrow."

Grever peered up at the rim of the pit to see two figures silhouetted against the sky. One was Gravis, the other Gaudere. He shrank back, appalled.

"Grever," his brother said, "I will be sending a rope ladder down –"

"No!" Grever's voice echoed around the pit. "Let her go first!"

Gravis shook his head. "She has committed a cardinal sin. Do you not realise why you survived this mine?"

"What are you talking about, you maniac?"

"She fired pure happiness at you," Gravis replied.

"I had to," Gaudere sobbed, "to stop him running into the mines –"

"*Silence,* you," Gravis said.

"Don't talk to her like that!" Grever cried. "Just because she's a woman. Leave her alone. I don't trust you for a moment, and I'm not coming up there to be captured by you."

"You must. I am your master –"

"What? You're my broth–"

"I am your *master* because I am the leader of the Sorrow Guild. You are subservient to me, the man. So you will do as you are told. I will let down the rope ladder, then you will climb it."

Grever felt the return of the self-destructive madness that he had glimpsed when the miner grasped his hand. "Never!" he said. "I'll never bow to you. *Man?* You don't even know what happens between men and women – d'you think nobody knows that? You're a dry husk, not my brother!"

Hearing this, Gravis seemed half strangled by fury, though his face told more of his struggle to contain the emotion than of the emotion itself. He flung the rope ladder over the side of the pit and shouted, "I'll come down there myself and get you." Then he turned to Gaudere, adding, "You first. I'm not leaving you up here."

Gaudere squeaked and knelt down by the top of the rope ladder.

Gravis cuffed her on the side of the head. "Get moving, woman."

"Leave her *alone!*" Grever shouted.

Gaudere began climbing down the rope ladder, Gravis following, just a few feet above her. Grever approached the bottom of the ladder and grabbed her as she alighted, then pulled her away before Gravis could jump to the pit floor.

By now a few more miners had entered the pit, so that an audience of half a dozen watched the struggle. Grever guided Gaudere to the opposite wall then hugged and kissed her. He said, "Don't worry my darling, I'll get you out of this."

"But Grever... I really did fire at you. I thought I'd lose you! You were going to run into the mines."

"I know – I was going to. I was mad with grief. But you saved me."

Gaudere glanced at Gravis then murmured, "Well, I'm not sure I did."

Grever looked at his brother, then raised his hand, palm out. "Stop there," he said.

"You will make me?" Gravis replied.

"If you don't stop, I'll tell everybody about your... you know."

Gravis halted. "My what?"

"What you are. Men and women. You know, *brother.*"

Gravis glanced at the miners, at Gaudere, then back at Grever. "You would not dare. Who is your loyalty to? Our family, is that it? Or to the greater purpose, which is the survival of the Sorrow Guild."

"*Sorrow* Guild?" Grever said. "You don't even know what sorrow is! You didn't shed a tear at the funeral. Why are *you* so great at leading, eh?"

"It is inappropriate for the Guildmaster of the Sorrow Guild to show emotion. It is undignified. The organisation has to be led by a calm, collected individual. You know that Grever, because you are our father's son. You saw how he conducted his affairs, did you not?"

"We're not talking about him, we're talking about you," Grever insisted. "I'll never do what you say. You've turned into an unfeeling monster. You don't know what emotion is. You've changed, and I don't like you any more."

"You sound like a little boy," Gravis sneered. "I am not having any more of this. Hand the woman back. You are both coming with me back to Sorgian, and then there wlll be punishment."

"You're a virgin, Gravis. A *virgin*."

The miners gasped. Gaudere gripped Grever's hand and squeezed it.

"You lie," Gravis said.

Grever turned to the miners. "Look at his face! You can see it's the truth. Even he can't hide the truth from showing on his face, though he's trying to."

"Grever, you lie," Gravis repeated.

"It's the truth. Look at your miners. They're laughing at you. Who's the big grand master now, eh? Who runs the guild and the mines? A virgin!"

A couple of the miners smirked, then stared at the floor, faces set.

Gravis took a revolver from his uniform pocket, aimed it at Gaudere, then fired.

Her body was flung against the pit wall by the force of the impact. Grever fell over. The miners scattered to the opposite side of the pit, where they reassembled, like a small army unit behind their captain. And Grever got to his feet to see them all staring at him.

Gaudere was down and bleeding, but she was alive. Grever made to kneel at her side.

Gravis squeezed the trigger a fraction. "Touch her," he said, "and you both die. Stand back, Grever. We all know what happens if happiness is brought into the Mines of Sorrow."

"Aye," the miners muttered to themselves. "'Tis contamination..."

Gravis pointed the revolver at Grever, his mind calculating angles, trajectories. He remained uncertain of the woman.

He had hoped to kill her outright, but she was still alive. It was important that the pair die swiftly so that the situation could be brought under control.

He understood now the vital function of the suit of armour. In the pit – almost like embodied spirits – the animal emotions of the others were assailing him, telling him to react, to *feel*. But he would not. To lead, to direct, to manage, he had to remain clear of mind and calm of body. He would *not* let the emotions of the moment direct events. He would lead as did any leader.

He took a deep breath. It was so much better to remain distant, so much easier. No man could lead an organisation as ancient and complex as the Sorrow Guild if he got his hands dirty.

He smiled. He approved of that one. His hands would remain clean.

He raised the gun and fired twice, once at Gaudere and once at Grever. A minute later both lay dead.

He turned to the miners. "You will say nothing of this," he said.

The miners said nothing in reply.

"It is Sorrow Guild policy never to allow contamination into the mines," he continued. "The substances of the Happiness Guild and our guild are intrinsically opposed – like black and white. Do you understand?"

Some of the miners nodded, but others shrugged. Then one said, "Will you be making a report to the Secretary, sir? To explain the bodies."

"Of course not," Gravis replied. "They will be buried in unmarked graves. By one of you, quite possibly. Then nothing more will be said."

"But what about the loss of your brother?" said another miner. "He'll be missed. Search parties will be led out of Sorgian."

Gravis did not grasp the point. "Search parties?" he queried.

The miner nodded. "He's your brother. He'll be missed...

tonight, I expect, when he doesn't come home for his supper. You need to take that into account, sir."

Gravis frowned. "I do not think you have assimilated my point," he said. "*Nothing* will be said about this – about the lie spoken by Grever, and about what I had to do in response to the contamination. The Sorrow Guild will continue unblemished. You six men will all say nothing for the rest of your lives. You are miners in the Mines of Sorrow. You are not ordinary men. You will do as I say."

"But sir, the people of Sorgian... our families... your mother. They'll want answers, won't they?"

Gravis made no reply. He realised there was only one option now. The other revolver in his pocket had not yet been fired. It contained six bullets.

# The Night of Red Butterflies

## Jessy Randall

We are in the city, crowded like macaroni in a casserole. Night time. Packs of people coming out of the restaurants and dance clubs. Drunkenness. Shouting. Occasional gunfire. The usual. And someone looks up, and suddenly everyone is looking up. Red neon butterflies up there, double triangles, little bow ties. Flickering and pointing at particular stars. And we all start rising up, floating up in groups. Euphoria. Gladness. Singing. People smiling like it's a giant birthday party and it's time to stuff ourselves with cake.

Except Grady. He's holding me down. He's making himself weigh extra, somehow. He's dragging on my hand, slowing our flight.

"Where do you think we're going?" he asks, all suspicious. Not joining in the fun. We're three or four storeys high, floating up to the butterflies.

"They're pointing us the way," I say. "They found a way to get us away from here!"

"Who's they?" says Grady. "And what if we want to stay?"

"Why would we want to stay?" I ask. We've stopped going up and are now sort of treading air, resting while other groups and pairs and singles rise around us. "Why in the hell would we want to stay here?" I ask him. He's spoiling everything. I want to go, go, GO...

But as the crowds fade my desire fades too. Why did I want to go? What exactly were those butterflies promising?

Grady didn't know what would happen if we went up – it was just his usual distrustfulness, his certainty that if everybody else was happy about something then he couldn't be. And so we stayed here, and found this house, all lit up that first night. And all twenty-six of you in it.

You've heard this part of the story a hundred times. You were on the main floor, all lined up in transparent bassinets, like the ones at a hospital. With labels saying your names and ages. You were hooked up to intravenous lines and big bottles of liquid. I think you all would have survived maybe a week without us. Just as well, since it took us almost that long to figure out how to do the feedings and the burpings and the diaper changes, just two of us and so many of you.

Close as we can figure, you're all the children of politicians and engineers and high-ups in NASA – big mucky-mucks who knew in advance about the red butterflies. No, before you ask again, we don't know what happened to them, or why the butterflies didn't affect you. No, we don't know what happened to all the other children. Or, I should say, we prefer not to think about it.

Anyhow, that's your story. Our story. The story we're still telling. And I expect we'll be telling it for at least a few more years, until you're all old enough not to ask for bedtime stories any more.

# Petrol-Saved

## Charles Wilkinson

Mr Tipley asked himself whether it was true that the postman who had just delivered a brown envelope had a metal hand. He had noticed at once that there was no name on the envelope. As he turned it over, only to discover that there was also no writing on the back, he was half aware of the postman hurrying away with his head bowed. Now he tried to recall the precise sequence of events: the doorbell ringing; the unbolting and opening; the postman standing there, his arm outstretched, the letter ready to be received. And then, just after he had shut the door, an image of a flash of rare Welsh sunlight, glinting on a hand that was not made of flesh. He told himself that he was mistaken. At the time he had been concentrating on the letter and not on the hand holding it. Perhaps the man had been wearing a watch with a metallic strap, which must have reflected the sunlight at the very instant that he had taken the letter. Mr Tipley took pride in having arrived at a rational explanation.

Ten minutes later, he stepped outside and into the Welsh weather: the sky, a diluted blue with the foam of thin white clouds; green-black forests covering the foothills, the separate spears of individual pine trees easily discernible; in the distance, the outline of the mountains – uncharacteristically clear. All this argued in favour of what passed for a fine day in the principality. Opposite him was a line of shops with lowering frontages, slate roofs and mean windows with frames that were painted black, and to his right a late Victorian town hall in machine-carved red brick topped by an incongruously small cupola. Beyond that stood a row of tall iron railings, rendered redundant by an enormous hedge, banked behind like a green thunderstorm. Iron gates, which were padlocked, discouraged entrance to a long gravel drive that led, Mr Tipley assumed, to a large house.

It was the beginning of the week, a day on which he had always attempted to muster a sense of purpose. But the fact that the little town had designated Monday as a lesser Sunday sapped any initiative he had felt whilst taking his solitary breakfast. He wore a hacking jacket of green tweed and magenta cords, but the weak Welsh sunlight failed to burnish his brown brogues, which he had worked on the previous night until they would have satisfied a Sandhurst sergeant-major.

The butcher's was only a few doors down from his own house. As always, there was no one behind the counter, although an assortment of chicken pieces, sausages, lamb chops and steaks had been laid out. There were two notices: one, propped between a side of beef and an enormous cooked ham, said *Carve Your Own*; the other, written on a filthy white-board in either blood or red felt tip, announced: *All meats to be paid for at Caradog's Coffee Shop*. Mr Tipley took a lamb chop, wrapped it in grease paper and made his way across the square. Although it was not early, there was no one about on the streets.

A bell rang as he stepped into the Coffee Shop and a bald man wearing overalls emerged from the back. He smelt of oil. Mr Tipley gave him the lamb chop and waited while he weighed it and then consulted a laminated price list that was hanging from a hook on the wall.

"I don't know why the prices aren't displayed in the butcher's shop," said Mr Tipley, paying him.

"Standard, that is."

"What do mean?"

"He don't live here, do he. So this is standard. Always has been."

"Well, it's most unusual as far as I'm concerned." As the

man turned towards the gloomy corridor at the back, Mr Tipley said quickly. "A pot of tea, if you please."

There was only one customer, apart from himself: an elderly man with white hair and tiny eyes, who was seated near the window, gazing disconsolately at the cobbled square and a stunted tree adjacent to an empty car park.

"Do you know of a good doctor around here?" Mr Tipley asked.

The man looked towards him as if he were observing something from a great distance.

"Thinking of going to the doctor, are you?" he replied at last.

"I'd like to make an appointment as soon as possible."

"I'd advise against it."

"I have a condition that needs looking at. Urgently."

"There's only one doctor round these parts."

"What's his name?"

"Drives a Chevrolet Convertible, he does."

"I asked you his name!"

The man stretched his fingers under the folds of flesh hanging from his jawbone as if he were trying to prevent his face from slipping onto the table like jelly.

"I couldn't be telling you that."

"Well, which surgery do you go to?"

He paused, looked out across the square and then down at his newspaper. "I don't be going to see no medical man," he muttered.

Once he had finished his tea, Mr Tipley took the tray back to the counter and peered into the dark corridor.

"Excuse me!"

The owner sauntered out, wiping his hands on greasy rag.

"Could you please recommend a doctor?"

"A doctor? Recommend a doctor?"

There was nothing on the counter except for one slice of lemon drizzle cake under a perspex cover.

"Surely there is a doctor in this town?"

"You said 'recommend'," replied the man, turning away and walking back down the corridor.

Outside, there had been a change in the weather: the western half of the sky was brewing blue-black thunder-clouds; the rain came in at a steep angle, bouncing off the cobblestones. What was left of the sunlight was hurrying off in the direction of Herefordshire. Mr Tipley had forgotten his umbrella. His thoughts turned to the contents of the envelope: a single sheet of white paper – a bill for five thou-sand and five hundred pounds. Neither the sender nor the addressee was named and there was no indication as to what services had been rendered: simply a column of figures, which had been added up correctly, and a statement to the effect that the account was to be paid in full within the next fourteen days. Evidently it had been delivered in error. But then there was the manner of its arrival. His earlier explana-tion now seemed unconvincing. He had never seen the postman before and was unable to remember the details of his appearance, apart from an impression that he was neither young nor old. And so why he did have such a clear recollection of the brown envelope and the metal hand holding it? Was it not possible, he argued, that he had not perceived the postman's hand as being made of metal at the moment that he had seen it, but later had somehow intuited that this was the case? He had just begun to consider ordering another cup of tea when the rain stopped and the sunlight flicked on, the clouds whipped away as if by a conjuring trick.

Mr Tipley had found his house three months previously whilst on a motoring holiday he had awarded himself in honour of his retirement from the small firm of Midland solicitors where he had worked for thirty years. He had been looking forward to buying a substantial house in the country and engaging in pursuits that were far removed from arranging the exchange of contracts for the sale of Indian restaurants or drawing up wills for elderly widows who had very little to leave. It was unfortunate that his wife, who had long tired of him, refused to leave her friends in the city. The subsequent divorce had left him with depleted financial resources and unable to afford the type of property that he had initially hoped to buy. Fortunately the marital home sold quickly and he decided to acquire a home on the Welsh Marches, where he had been told houses were cheap.

The day that he set out for the town was one of hurrying rainstorms tugged by westerlies, swirling blue-grey clouds replaced by sudden, sunlit escapades; frothing mists blurring escarpments; and then just as he crossed the border into Wales, a sky that was half blue, half grey with a hoop of rainbow hovering above a watery green.

As he drove into the town fifteen minutes later, a crosswind wind was hurling water across the square, which seemed to be tilting like the deck of a ship in high seas. The wind streamed across the choppy cobbles and buffeted the huddled shops. He parked the car and searched in the back seat for the estate agents' brochures. By the time he surfaced the storm had vanished and he saw at once an elegant Georgian townhouse with sash windows, its façade painted the shade of lemon ice-cream; it had a small garden filled with geraniums and roses behind freshly painted blue railings. A building that was in striking contrast to the low-browed cottages and sombre little shops that surrounded it. A splash of colour beside grey slate and stone. The sunlight seemed to have selected it, an illuminated place in a dour Welsh day.

He had not thought he had the funds to buy a period property, but the house was cheap. With half the money from the sale of his home in the city, he could afford it on condition that he managed to sell a tiny flat that he had inherited from an aunt and let out to produce an additional income. The tenancy was due to expire in the spring and then he would put it on the market. With the aid of a bridging loan, and without bothering to ask for a structural survey, he was able to complete his purchase less than six weeks after he had first seen the house on that afternoon of rain and elusive, scampering sunlight.

But today he was beginning to wonder if he had been too hasty. Before signing the contract, he had paid little attention to the location. A quick stroll around the town had confirmed his impression of it as a typical border town that had lost its market and whatever small industries that it must once have had. Now that he had looked around it more carefully he realised that it lacked most of the amenities commonly considered essential to any conurbation of the same size in the West Midlands. There was a chapel that had been converted into a charity shop, a large garage, a place that repaired bicycles, one coffee shop and three public houses that appeared to be permanently closed, but no Post Office, school, newsagent's, dentist, vet, church, library, hairdressers, launderette or pharmacist.

One Saturday afternoon he found a network of narrow lanes behind the Town Hall. This quarter was reserved in the mediaeval manner for one trade. All of the shops, and there must have at least twenty of them, were what Mr Tipley classified as hardware stores or ironmongers, although these terms were not adequate to describe a number of subsidiary activities that took place on the premises. Nearly all of them had supplies of spare parts for washing machines, lawnmowers, motorcycles, even motor cars. Customers came in quest of camshafts, connecting rods, flywheels or propflanges. This merchandise was often bartered rather than sold. Mr Tipton found the proprietors of these concerns largely uncommunicative, prepared only to discuss the merits of whatever type of battery or light bulb he had expressed an interest in purchasing.

There was also a more pressing matter: the difficulty of finding a doctor who could attend to his condition. One day when he was at home consulting the Yellow Pages in order to see if there was a practice somewhere in the area, the phone on the table by the front window rang. Mr Tipley was surprised to hear the voice of his financial adviser.

"Ah Tipley," the man said, once the initial pleasantries had been completed. "Glad to get hold of you at last. I've got some rather unwelcome news for you about your bridging loan."

"Oh?"

"It's probably nothing to be worried about at all, but since it is a little irregular I thought I should let you know at once. You remember that you took out the loan with the One Life Building Society."

"Of course."

"Well, I've now been told that the loan has been bought by a man called Jouissaint... What's rather odd is that he lives in your neck of the woods. Have you come across him at all?"

"No. I've never even heard of him. Listen Meredith, are they allowed to do this?"

"Not only are they allowed to do so, they are required to take this step. Apparently there is a bylaw in your part of the principality that says that debts can only be owed to this man Jouissaint. If anybody has an outstanding debt to someone else, then within eight weeks of it having been incurred it must be bought by Jouissant. It all sounds positively feudal to me, but there you are. Anyway, I don't expect that it will make very much difference. There's been no attempt to change the terms."

"I am surprised that One Life didn't take the trouble to write to me about this."

"They did. And so did I. That's why I'm ringing now."

"Well I haven't had either of the letters. Mind you the postal service does seem to be somewhat idiosyncratic around here. I had a strange bill the other day. It arrived in an envelope with a stamp on it but nothing else. I'm not even sure that it was for me."

"Who was it from?"

"It didn't say. It was simply a bill for five thousand five hundred pounds. You couldn't check the amount due on the mortgage, could you? Perhaps it has something to do with that."

It was raining again, so heavily that the far side of the square was only just visible.

"I'll let you know," said Meredith. "It's not worth losing any sleep over, but I'm sure you understand that I had to inform you of this change."

"Yes, of course. Thanks for ringing. Oh, you haven't got this chap Jouissaint's address by any chance?"

"Not to hand. I'll pop it in the post when it turns up."

He put the phone down. The wind threw a sheet of water across the glass so that for a moment the outside world disappeared and the dark lines around the panes stood out like rigging. Outside the weather changed from minute to minute, but his condition remained constant. He imagined himself stretching his hands out, trying to crawl up towards the crow's-nest, as if from there he could escape from himself in the boundless sky.

After a month, the westerlies were packed away for a week, stored safely out sea where the worst gales blew. Every day the sky was a sheet of pale blue, close to the shade of Wedgewood china, but with an ice-rink sparkle. Unfamiliar bright sunlight fell into Mr Tipton's room and woke him early. He dressed hurriedly and polished his shoes, whose leather had dulled lately, to a high gleam. Today he would find the doctor's surgery and demand a cure for his condition; then he would discover where Jouissaint lived.

At nine o'clock he stepped out on to the square.

"Morning," said a man. His white coat was covered in blood and he held a raw carcass under his left arm.

"Ah, at last, my neighbour the butcher," said Mr Tipton, following the man into his shop. "Although you may not realise it, I'm a regular customer of yours."

"They tells me you come in, they do. New man in the Jouissaint's town house, they says."

"As a matter of fact, I've bought the property. Admittedly with the aid of a small loan."

"Bought it, have you?" replied the man. "Well, there's been some who've said similar, I'll grant you that."

"This Mr Jouissaint. I believe I have some business with him. But I haven't been able to find out where he lives."

"No surprise that. They're close round here. Very close. I live off, you see, and so that's why I can tell you that his place is over there."

The man pointed to the iron gates.

"It looks as if it's a large property if those hedges mark the extent of it."

"I couldn't say. I've never delivered there. I'm from off, and that's the way I likes to keep it."

He cut the beef into portions, arranged some joints on the counter next to the cooked ham and then glanced at his watch.

"I'm grateful to you for being so forthcoming. As you rightly say, the people round here appear very reserved by nature. I've been quite unable to find out where the surgery is even though it has been strongly implied that a doctor does live here."

"He does."

"Oh where?"

"Same place." Once again, the man pointed in the direction of the iron gates and the overgrown hedge.

"So Jouissant is a doctor."

"That's been said. Although whether he is a medical man in the strict sense of the term I couldn't tell you."

"How many are there in the practice?"

"Just Dr Jouissant."

"Are you by any chance a..."

"A patient!" the man wiped his bloody hands on his long white coat. "No one from off would be one of his patients. Though I've heard it said that his powers of restoration are quite remarkable. You'll be a new man if you go to him, you will. Not that I'm advising that, mind. I ain't one for all this being built again."

"Built again?"

"That's what they calls themselves. Built again."

Once the pleasure of paying the butcher in his own shop was over, Mr Tipton decided to take a quick walk around the town. The iron gates were still shut and so there was no point in searching for the surgery. But as he walked towards the town hall, he noticed that a large sign had been erected at the bottom of the steps; it said: "Welcome to the Black Scarp Vintage Car Association."

The first driver arrived shortly before noon. The dark leather of his coat and broad-rimmed hat almost matched the black bodywork of his Bugatti. The outline of the buildings, along with the window frames, the pattern of the brickwork and the roof-tiles, stood out in the clarity of the winter sun. An absence of shadows made the town look as if it were a cut-out pasted onto a dreamy backdrop of wooded hills and blue-glass sky that had been painted earlier by another hand. The driver got out of his car and looked around the square. He was tall but preternaturally thin. Mr Tipley tried to imagine how slender the man's neck must be under the folds of his charcoal scarf.

At lunchtime The Raven, The Black Eagle and The Hooded Monk opened their doors. Cars arrived steadily. Sometimes alone, sometimes in threes or fours; the streets filled with ancient Rileys, Austins, Armstrong Sidleys, Alvises and even a Frazer Nash. Drinkers spilled out on to the steps of The Raven. Some with goggles and jackets lined with sheepskin had the appearance of aviators or racing drivers from an earlier age. A smell of exhaust hung in the air.

Mr Tipley followed a group into the quarter behind the Town Hall. The narrow streets were filled with unaccustomed movement. Everywhere drivers were inspecting crankcases, connecting rods and hub caps. On the pavements were boxes heaped with oily parts. A funnel was being fitted to an empty can, which a driver held steady whilst petrol was poured in. The customary silence of the quarter had been replaced by a polyphony of voices in which words and whole phrases seemed on the point of achieving intelligibility before being subsumed in a wave of sound. Even when Mr Tipley stood right next to two men, who appeared to be debating the merits of a tail pipe, he was quite unable to identify a single word with any degree of certainty, although the texture of their speech was that of language known to him.

It would be helpful, Mr Tipley decided, to find out where the rally was taking place, but most of the people around him seemed to be too busy for him to disturb them with impunity. He was about to leave the quarter when he noticed the solitary driver, who had been the first to reach the town, coming towards him. Now that he was closer he saw that he was both taller and even thinner than he had originally thought. His leather coat almost reached his ankles and the scarf covered not only his neck, but the bottom half of his face. His skin was impossibly pale, on the verge of translucency. Then just too late, he saw that next to the man's nose, which had the sharp line of a mathematical instrument, was a single eye the shade of diesel. There was a pit of scar tissue with a metal cross where the other pupil had been. Mr Tipley had already stepped into the man's path. Moving back now would have betrayed the repulsion he felt at the man's appearance.

"Excuse me," he said, "I was wondering if you could possibly tell me where the rally is to be held?"

Very carefully the man unwound his scarf. The elements of the lower half of his face – his lips, his teeth, the line of his jagged jaw – had been welded together from disparate sheets of metal. His neck was still flesh, although close to the windpipe was a small hole ringed with stainless steel, a place for topping up the darkness within.

At dusk the iron gates opened. Mr Tipley watched from his living-room window. While there was a pink glow above the hills, it was still possible to make out the vintage cars, as they made their way along the road by the hedges and turned left into the driveway. Night fell. All he could see were the rear lights following each other. It was odd that the rally had been arranged so that it would take place in darkness. After his attempt to question the tall motorist, Mr Tipley had inquired in several of the shops, but found both customers and owners evasive. Yet at least one of them had implied that the rally would be held in the grounds of Dr Jouissaint's house.

It seemed likely that the gates would remain open until the event was over, but Mr Tipley decided against taking the risk. His condition had continued to worsen. If there was a surgery in the town, there was only one place where it could be. No doubt Dr Jouissant would be occupied with the rally. Nevertheless, there was no reason, Mr Tipley assured himself, why he shouldn't drop off a request for an appointment.

He put on his overcoat and made his way down to the iron gates. The road was lined with trees on both sides, and although the stars were out Mr Tipley was glad that he had bought a torch with him. No house could be seen, and not a car passed him as he made his way towards a bend in the drive. The only sound was a faint susurration in the undergrowth, some small animal passing innocuously through the ferns. The moon's grey maria were clearly visible on a watery milk background.

As soon as he rounded the corner, he came to a standstill. The façade of the house in front of him was lit up by floodlights, but there was no illumination in any of the windows; even the porch was in darkness. No cars were parked in front of the house. Mr Tipley now became aware of the sound of engines, rising and falling continuously. For a moment, it seemed that the noise was not that of machines being raced around a track but of mechanical beasts in

pursuit of some unnamed quarry. At times the constant roar
rose to a snarl and the screech of the brakes seemed to
merge with the pitiful, almost human squeal of tyres.

Mr Tipley made his way across the gravel forecourt. He
was surely more likely to find the surgery tucked away at the
rear of the building. There was no lighting along the side of
his house, but to his left he could make out a sunken tennis
court. He directed his torch downwards. The grass immediately below him was covered with the remains of motor cars.
Some had been stripped down to the bare bones of the
chassis; others had lost little more than their wheels;
around them was a glittering sea of mechanical parts.

He found the surgery at the back. It was housed in a long
low outbuilding that might once have been used as a garage.
Although there was no sign, he could tell from the ramp
that it had evidently been built to allow wheel-chair access.
Lights were on in the two windows nearest to the entrance.
He turned off his torch and pushed the door; it opened
soundlessly to reveal a waiting-room. Chairs had been
placed against the wall and there was an unoccupied recep-
tion desk. Next to it was a hatch with drawn shutters that
Tipton presumed concealed a dispensary. There were
framed photographs of vintage cars on the walls. He walked
past the hatch and along a small corridor. The door at the
end was slightly open. A red light flickered on the wall and
as he edged closer he was aware of the steadily increasing
heat, the proximity of the flame, the scent of soldering and
hot metal, the stink of God's petroleum. At once he understood he had come to the place of remaking. Now he could
see the sparks. This was the workshop where the body was
stripped down, the bones rebuilt, the nails machined, the
mouth and the teeth milled, the skull chamfered, the
fingers turned, the arteries welded to the heart's steel pump,
readied for the fuel of life reborn as darkness.

Meredith drove away from the city and its suburbs and west
into an afternoon of green-gold shadow-leaf, along lanes

steeped in the dark honey that glows at sundown; through villages with ancient-angled cottages in black and white. It was a nuisance, but he had to find out what had happened to Tipley. First, there was the business over One Life, and now the failure to respond to repeated requests to get in touch with the office.

When Meredith reached the border, he was an hour away from nightfall and leaving the fine day behind. He could see the clouds holding black water over the foothills; and then the first mist of rain drifting over high copses and the pine forest beyond.

It had been three weeks since he had heard from Tipley. A buyer had been found for the flat, but letters and phone calls had gone unanswered, and so Meredith had been forced to step in. And there was the matter of the bridging loan. Meredith had received a message from Dr Joussaint informing him that the debt had been discharged, but no money had been taken from Tipton's account. All attempts to contact Joussaint had been as unproductive as the attempts to communicate with Tipley.

Spots of rain formed like Braille on the windscreen, along with the sense that if he were to close his eyes and stretch out his hand he could touch the truth of the weather, feel the words emerging from blindness clearer than anything he could ever see. Then he realised that he was lost. The landscape beyond the windscreen changed as he drove deeper into the hills. Now rain blurred the dots; the wipers dissolved the road and the forest then stretched them back into semi-clarity for a second or so. Had he missed the turning a mile back? He braked and took out a map. When he looked up the rain had stopped as suddenly as it had started. The town was marked and yet now the geography outside the car seemed to bear little relation to what was in the grid. It was as if the relevant grey snake of road had slithered back into the undergrowth with a hiss. Then just as he was about to go back to the nearest village to ask for directions, he saw the sign; he was almost there.

As he drove into the town, he noticed one beautiful house, so much lighter than the surrounding grey terraces that it was as if it had its own store of sun. He was sure that this was Tipley's house, but just after he had parked in front of it a man wearing a stained apron came out of a butcher's shop. Meredith wound down a window.

"Looking for Mr Tipley, are you?" said the man, leaning towards the car. His jaw and throat were speckled with tiny droplets of dried blood.

"Yes."

"Well, you won't find him here."

"Oh? I thought that this was his house."

"Not any longer. They have taken him up to the garage, haven't they? Over there." The man pointed to an unprepossessing barn of a building built out of timber and corrugated iron.

"Thank you, for your help," said Meredith, getting out of his car. It wasn't far to walk; in fact, he could already hear a faint hammering, along with an even more distant rise and fall of voices, chapel-like, half-way between speech and song.

The door was open. To his surprise, the sounds, which had not increased in intensity as he approached the building, stopped the instant he crossed the threshold. Silence. The scent and smart of petrol seemed to hang in the air: a miasma stinging his eyes. He blinked and looked around. As far as he could tell, there was no one there. The remains of ancient automobiles covered the uneven mud floor. Some were supported by small towers of bricks; others had the look of having been abandoned part way through the ritual of restoration.

"Tipley?"

Meredith made his way deeper into the building, weaving past empty jerry cans, piles of wrenches and anonymous steel parts that had the oily glint of fish. Then he saw him. Tipley was in a torpedo-shaped sidecar, where from a distance he appeared to be resting as if he were comfortable in his chrysalis of steel. The vehicle he was attached to looked to be hardly more than a chassis. All the doors, the hood and bonnet had gone. But though stripped of its musculature of bodywork and chrome, it still had its metal frame. The driver's wheel seemed incongruously large, but there was no seat left from which to look at the engine beneath. As Meredith moved closer, he noticed Tipley's eyes were open. There was no expression in them. Repairs had recently been made to his face; the mouth and jaw had the sheen of fresh aluminium. He was still wearing his tweed jacket: the thin blue lines on the green jacket were a memory of rivers and fields.

It wasn't until Meredith was only a foot away he understood that below the waist Tipley had been merged with the substance of the sidecar, the lower half of his body tapering like a metal mermaid. The engine was idling, almost inaudibly. Tipley shifted his head slightly. The jacket sleeve nearest to the vehicle had been drawn up, exposing an arm that was still formed of flesh. A stent pierced his wrist, from which a long cord, glistening umbilically, stretched to the tank that was feeding Tipley, dripping enough black joy to drive his new heart.

# Wild Seed

## Ross Gresham

The seed hit the planet like a bullet into a dune. For a dead world, this was a notable moment. A geyser of dust jetted up, a column that was taken by the air, smoothed to a plume, then to a tattered, loose-vane feather. Then even that was gone, folded and dispersed into a hundred of the world's dust ghosts. Nothing more. One of the universe's unmarked events.

But give the robot seed its moment. The impact helped. It cracked a two-metre plate of mica. Below that was sand, and the roots pressed down. They could have been tree roots except that they delved straight, and when they bent, they bent at precise angles. In six hours a stem began to rise above the surface, though it didn't declare much: two metres, a rickety antenna, a mere willow wand, with leaves that were ribbons of grey film.

The roots went down, the stem went up, with a haste nature couldn't match, like three years of tree growth captured in stop-motion photography. But by then the machine had largely spent itself. To go on, it needed energy. It needed material. Could it find it?

It spent a pulse or two on brainwork. The possibilities for solar energy were limited. The wind could snap the stem – hollow, inferior metal – strip it of leaves, bury it in a dune... The seed brain determined that the real chance was down, where the soil itself held a faint, mysterious charge, like plunging into a vast weak battery, and also the promise of heat. Down. That was how the seed invested the last of its stores. Wires plunged.

The roots took what they needed. The metals to coat themselves, the energy to continue. They harvested the iron, flushed the silicon in flakes from the antenna. The iron hardened their xylem and phloem, thickened the stem, so that they might withstand against a freak gust.

It was enough. The growth was alive – or functioning. It had done better than most seeds. In a few decades, who knows? It might declare itself secure, and begin to think about extra, a useful project. It would assess what was available. It might start work on the atmosphere. Or start dropping fruit of refined metal. Whatever seemed best.

Eighteen months later, a kilometre below the surface, a hair-like wire found something it couldn't identify. Its cells discussed the matter, to the extent that they could. Their existence had been scratch, scratch, barely alive, barely the energy to think a single thought in a day. Now all at once that changed. Energy flowed like a river. Conservation concerns were dismissed, the brain awoke to build itself to its full, smoking capacity. It discussed this new richness. What had it found? What would it do with it? And already a new voice was entering into the conversation.

"As per contract, then, this clinic does possess a HH license, verified as you can see 8-8-67. Milgram, as holder of your original indenture, has taken the initiative to schedule the procedure, but this assistance implies no obligation on the part of Milgram or our shareholders, nor alteration nor flexibility to the pre-agreed payment schedule. As per contract, the procedure is undertaken by the clinic at the liability level you pre-arrange..."

These legalities don't interest the old man either, but he must walk through each, pausing until I make some minimal nod for his recording. I make these nods on cue and entertain the wild thought of killing him.

Debt wears you down. You smile and sign and pretend this all ends how? With a final payment and a handshake?

My regular defaults have inspired Milgram and Milgram,

Bank 18 in the overall standings, to fit me with a collar. That's why their representative is here in my office, to arrange the procedure.

This collar would live off me at minimal drain. I would go on the same as ever. Doing scientific consulting. Terraforming consulting. I do it by the day. I do it by the hour. Hell, I'd do it by the quarter hour, barely time to change the sheets, if I had any clients.

A collar, though. A servant's collar... Across the desk the old lawyer plays with his necktie. Does he sense what I'm thinking? That it's time to sever his head from his shoulders? A servant's collar can decapitate, this collar they plan to fit me with – it has cables that can tighten and pinch down to the size of a coin.

Of course that almost never happens. There's the math protecting you. Dead, I would be worth about 4500, though I'm deteriorating, and I probably appear to be worth much less. Legal frictions, testate, would reduce that by 300 or so, even for Milgram and Milgram. Death by strangulation would reduce that further. It would crush all those valuable, harvestable pipes and nerves in my neck, and that intricate column of bone. So maybe 2300, then?

In all, I owe fourteen million to Milgram and several other Banks.

Other Banks. His eyes occasionally flick to my left hand, wrapped in a black headscarf. I've already got a cuff there, sipping away, biding its time. That's from Micon Bank, and they're not happy. Their ranking is in the 40s, and they're insecure. The cuff has been quiet. Dormant. It's been saving up energy for something big. I wrap it with the headscarf because I'm sick of it watching me all the time – not to hide it from the Milgram representative. He came in and I was injecting glucose into my palm, a sort of sentimental gesture to keep the hand alive, now that the cuff is restricting the flow of nutrition. The horse syringe is out on the desk, where it's leaked a sticky puddle. No, Milgram knows all about the cuff. That's why they want the collar. It prioritizes their debt.

The old man's voice has stopped droning. I give a little nod so he can resume. Then I make a more pronounced nod. But he's not waiting on concurrence. His nose is wrinkled, and in a moment I get it too, a gust of air like brewed garbage. A suit is venting.

They are behind him in the hall. Two homesteaders. He must have left the security door propped. Probably he stationed a bodyguard in the hallway. Of course he did. Now I have two wandering homesteaders in the office.

"Clients," I mumble. "Cash clients."

Right. You could tell immediately they were homesteaders. One standard, one suited. Of course they had disregarded the sign about suits, and there it was, leaking its putrid gas. And if that didn't give them away, the one who showed her face, she had that dopey expression that comes from not living around people. It's not even an expression, it's expressionless. As though she's staring at some wall built three feet in front of her face.

Believe me. Twelve years I spent in an indenture orphanage. And I'd done my time in the outer planets. I knew what went with that expression. Body odour, and proud of it. Belief in simple truths. Simpleton. Simple virtues. Though if they suddenly decided that their God of Crops needed appeasement, you'd be up on a meat hook.

Also, no money. Homesteaders have no money.

"Lucrative clients," I say. "Big big."

The homesteader without the mask talks. She says, "Have you made room in your life for the living planet?"

The Milgram man lowers his head with a sigh. "Well then. Well then." Just like that he's packing his briefcase. He's miffed, like anyone would be if you cut short their appointment. But his own fault if he's going to prop the door for random street preachers.

To leave, he has to shuffle this way and that. The homesteaders don't even know how to move out of his way. The one with the face watches him with a fish mouth, no change in her dull, uncouth expression.

But get this, the Banker tips his hat to them. Like they're ladies in a receiving line. "Good day to you. Good day." What's sweet is that he even does it for the gal in the suit. You know with those methane suits, that's like tipping your hat to someone blowing farts.

Just like that he's gone. Just a harmless old man with a job to do. Good job, banking job, working for Milgram and Milgram. Ran my orphanage. No evil, no malice. Beautiful manners. A minute ago I fantasized about cutting off his head with a hacksaw.

Whew. Well, given this reprieve, I hop up and start packing. Sure, I've been hiding some money. Eight thousand saved up in fuel futures. I'll see if I can cash them out. See how far 8000 can get me.

I spare the girls a glance. Probably twins, one born with a body for their world, one born with a body for mine. They'd be swapping that suit their whole lives, without a lot of washing between.

"You're Doctor Vanson," says the unsuited one. "Eminent consultant in planetary science."

Doctor? Eminent consultant? No one has used my title in long time. Makes me blink, but my mind quickly moves to the only relevant questions: Clients? Any chance of money? Answers: No, no. "Come back tomorrow, ladies. Come back tomorrow. Got a climate problem? We'll clear it right up."

"You've heard of a wild seed?"

"Wild seed? Wild seed. Yeah. Luddite myth. If it's malfunctioning, tell it to stop."

"But doctor, it will not be commanded."

Nothing important to pack up, just a few screens. "Well, what did you try? Smoke signals? Give it a few pulses. Seeds don't have energy to chat." The suit girl doesn't move. Hasn't moved the whole time. That and the smell, could be she is dead in there. Maybe the suit carries her around as some homesteader religious totem.

The other one, the talking one, for some reason she is trying to help me pack. She's looking around for things to put in my duffle bag. She's found my hacksaw, and this so mystifies her that I have to take it from her grasp. "For my wrist," I tell her quietly. Toss it in on some papers. "The cuff. At some point, I'll amputate." On top of the saw, I throw in the tourniquet, just a pipe and a pants belt.

My best bet is to get off planet. For 8000 I may be able to bribe my way past perimeter security at the spaceport. I could stow-away on an ore ship, maybe clear this whole chapter of my life with just some radiation hair loss. I'll need a run of luck.

The live homesteader stands frozen, though her eyes still glance around for ways to help me. Poor girl. Did they have to cut their hair like that? Is there a homesteader instruction book somewhere with this helmet pattern? Is three snips with a scissor really that much more efficient than five or ten?

"Wh-when will the cuff maim you?"

She looks me straight in the eye. I was thinking she was damaged, so stupid that she needed diapers. But it's the tourniquet that shocked her.

I shrug. "That's the gall of it, lady. Who knows? It's someone else's decision. It's their whim. That's how I live now."

"Human flesh cannot be bought and sold."

A dangerous sentiment to articulate, even for a simpleton homesteader. "I'll make a note."

"Doctor. Sir, we come from the Plaxis system."

"Yeah?" I stop. That was mine. My old territory. Seeded that whole solar system.

The room fans come on. They smelled the suit and turned themselves up. Meanwhile, the talking girl is trying to say more, her jaw working up to the effort. In my orphanage there was a girl with a stutter. At some point she disappeared. Tiny thing. When she talked, was it better to help finish her sentence or to wait? I never knew.

The homesteader lady gets it out all at once: "Listen to me. Your mother's name was Lakme."

I drop my eyes. As though they might reveal something, as though they might glance to a family photograph on the wall, as though I might own such a picture, as though a picture of my mother might exist.

I wait a moment so as to speak carefully. "A seed... you give it a whole mindprint. In case it survives, it has to be able to think. The intent is cognitive abilities. But there's always some slop. Unattached data. Private memories. They're just chaff. They aren't whole or useful."

She is watching my face with odd intensity. Also disappointment. It's bizarre. You'd think I was telling her the hard truth about Santa. "Look, lady, seeds are a dead business. The Court ruled that they can't stake a territory claim. Got it? It has to be you. It has to be homesteaders, live humans. If you live there on the ground, the planet's yours. If you give birth one time, one live birth. That's what the Court ruled." My voice has an edge. But it's not this girl's fault. "If one of my old seeds is bothering you, sending odd data, dig it up. Kill it. It's a dead business. It cost me everything." I tap my wrapped hand on the desk. "Look, I've got to go, I'm out of time."

Sometime in my little speech, she produced a paper, and that's on the desk now. Again her chin trembles over some words. Rather than make her struggle, I give it a look. It's the curled print of an orbital photograph.

I say, "This can't be." It's like a painting, an artist's dream. It's an entire planet with a metal skin, shining like burnished nickel.

"The world is alive. It asked for you." Her eyes move – to my bag, the door, the wrap. Her eyes aren't looking, they're talking. She is pointing out my predicament. With no trouble at all, she says clearly: "We have a ship. Our launch window opens in twenty minutes."

I've been through the Bend so many times that I've probably lived here a week of my life. But a week measured how? By heartbeats? The Bend plays hell with clocks. Technically, you don't exist. You're lost in the fold.

But inside a craft you don't notice anything exceptional, except the quiet. Serious quiet. The only thing comparable is to walk through a forest when wet snow is falling. Wet, heavy snow, which makes no sound itself, and mutes away the sounds of the world.

In the central chamber the talking girl sits as though waiting. She sits before a sort of altar, with three large dishes of food. The light is two wax candles. She looks up.

"I owe you a debt," I say.

She indicates a chair. There is a second chair opposite hers.

She hasn't responded correctly, so I prompt her: "You may dictate the terms of my debt."

Her hair is pinned up on one side of her head. Wounded? Bandaged? No, she is trying to look pretty. She is pretty. Her dopey expression is gone, replaced by its opposite, severity. She's pulled her hair up tight as wire.

I sit. The plate before me is empty. Perhaps it's a symbol of my obligation. I am to watch her eat a meal? But the plate before her is empty as well. "Serve," she says.

"I will. Of course. Any legal request."

"I mean, help yourself to the food."

"I am to choose one of these dishes?"

"These are for us."

I've heard of this. We share some from each bowl. Beside my plate are several utensils to choose between. These we don't share. Manners – there are set manners for such an occasion, but I've had no practice in them. "I can't," I say finally, having touched each utensil for weight. "I don't know... I've been feeding through a stent. Whatever you don't choose, I'll eat the remnants. Happily."

She sighs. She serves food from each bowl onto my plate, then hers.

The plate isn't even sectioned. The food begins to mix promiscuously, though I try to prevent this with my tools. "Misdemeanour crime," I mutter. "To eat communally."

When she eats, I eat. When she chooses one of the foods, I eat that as well. The silence is enough to hear a candle flame. Only in the Bend.

My cuff squawks, cutting the mood. It's been squawking whenever it can work up the energy. It's already heavily wrapped, but I wrap it again. As part of the table service, there is a cloth provided for each of us. Using my teeth to hold a corner, I tie this around to add to the wadding. It's okay because the cloth is superfluous to the eating ritual. From the start the lady set hers aside in her lap.

A few words still come through comprehensibly. Vile, vulgar stuff. "Sorry," I mumble. "Beg your pardon."

"... evil." she says quietly.

I cinch the wrappings and bite back a response.

She clears her throat. "I say that what they've done to your hand is evil."

"Pre-recorded," I say, dismissively. "Standard stuff. When the cuff goes out of range."

"But not evil, to your mind."

"That's a fairly primitive vision of the world. Good, evil."

"Oh?"

"No one volunteers to pay. In the end, ugly things may happen."

"They are responsible for the consequences of their actions."

On the carefully arranged table, my hand is a clumsy padded club. "Who is responsible for this, if not me?"

"Who? Whatever Bank has stencilled its name on the device." She sets down her fork. "Distance from the consequences doesn't absolve you of them. Wilful ignorance of consequences doesn't absolve you – putting up fences until you can't see who you're harming."

"Ah, so simple." One advantage to this method of eating is that I have an excuse to lower my eyes. Why say more? From the start I recognized her calmness, the calmness of the zealot. All life conforms to some simple system.

It's my fault for talking to her, and I should stop, unless I wanted to hear more homespun homilies, memorized from the needlepoints hung round the walls of some home-steader pod.

She says, "For three years your voice has been talking to us, urging us to live most nobly. Me you saved from mind-less vengeance. You brought holiness to the conflict that engulfed my heart. My sister – she reveres you to such an extent that she can't bear to be in your presence. She thinks you're a god." Her voice grates. "To see the living man so pathetic, fearful and skittish, a mere lick-spittle..."

Impossible not to be disturbed, to find oneself the object of sincere disgust. Yet the only response I can summon is to shake my head in bafflement. She carries on: "You said – you told us so many things. You said, 'A fat man eating quails while children are begging for bread is a disgusting sight, but you are less likely to see it when you are within sound of the guns.'"

"That's not me."

She winces.

"It's Eric Blair. George Orwell," I say. "Important writer. Yes. Could have been in my mindprint. So. The seed really wastes energy giving speeches?"

"The world speaks. You saw the image of it."

Shaking my head. "Fake image. You're being fooled... Gulled... A seed couldn't..."

"Not just any seed. One of yours. You. The most eminent climate engineer who has ever lived."

I doubletake, but she intends no irony. This woman seems incapable of it. "Perhaps we should say 'at one point the most promising...'"

"The most eminent scientist... Abandoned to an indenture orphanage, age two, yet you climbed out of that slave hole. Read everything. Learned everything. The most eminent scientist." She returns to her snarl. "Now look at you. Content to have a device eating your hand."

I respond quietly. "Certainly it tries. For punishment or nourishment – who can decide?"

She takes hold of my elbow. I pull away as she begins to unwrap. "You say you owe me a debt. Very well, I require your submission."

Soon the hand is bare. Famine has made it feminine. Blue, and bruised with injection marks. One has to pity it.

She touches the yellow, finds the needle marks. "Injecting? You resist its sanction, though apparently you find it legitimate."

"No reason to mock," I say. "I don't resist because I *can't* resist. I mean, I can't stop the feed. Only delay the inevitable." It's been some time since I've looked upon the cuff, the black coil of it. It has the ominous presence of a handgun. An oily serpent. By way of excuse I offer, "And they chose my left hand. I play the violin."

She rubs at the dying flesh with disgust. "Does the irony move you at all, that you developed the technology for its feeding?"

"Not the vampiric exchange," I snap. "Only the heat plate. Not the nutrients. A thousand better methods suggest themselves immediately. Lady, who the hell are you? Ouch."

"Ah!" Her face is suddenly gleeful. "My goodness, what could be the matter?"

"The cuff. We're coming out of the Bend."

The cuff isn't designed for Bending, and it heats up in the friction. She loves this. She stretches both her hands around the black metal, exhilarated by the burn. "Oh yes. Oh yes we are." Her gaze holds mine. "Does that worry you? Do you worry that you won't escape after all? That your device will call your poor creditors and inform them where you've gone?"

"I wish it would try, lady. The effort would cost it too much. Any message, just a single pip, would leave it helpless. In a moment I'd have it off with a cold chisel."

As we pass out of the Bend, there's a moment of disorientation. That's all, and we're back in the world of clocks.

I blink to restore my equilibrium. One quick blink but she's leaned in across the table. I draw back. Looks like she's trying to bite my hand. But she has a firm grip on my elbow.

It's the cuff, the searing cuff. She leans close, inhaling, sniffing it. Speaking into it with utter clarity, she says, "My name is Sara Foyle."

"Oh."

The cuff goes dead. Spent itself. Sent its message. It is a dead thing on my wrist.

Sara Foyle. Her colony was starved. Rather, they were denied access to the marketplace. They starved. But there was no responsible agent. The Court was petitioned and made its ruling.

It was after this incident that her name became known. Sara Foyle took a different view of liability. She was clever, and somehow acquired a Bend ship. Many thousands had died by her machinations. Four Banks were driven completely out of the standings. Sara Foyle. I didn't even believe she was real. She was so vilified, I assumed she was a myth.

Sara Foyle leads me to the flight deck. Her sister is there in the suit. The legs on the suit are impossibly thin. I see that now. What small bit of her could still be alive?

At once we see the nickel planet. It's enormous. Its eminence lights the cabin. I remember the place. It was rock and sand. Huge, but not very promising. Poison atmosphere. A long shot. Gave it a half dozen seeds, an afterthought, each calculated with a mere 8% chance of surviving the first year.

"He has taken us in its arms," says the suit. She's enraptured. We're being embraced by the planet's gravity and she's joyous about it. We came in foolishly close. You can't Bend if you're in this sort of gravity.

The surface of the planet is built completely. It has grown a skin of polished metal. This has never happened and in fact cannot happen. Shapes and angles jut out. Spike mountains. I say, "It's not my mind, Sara. It's familiar, but it's not a product of my mind."

Sara is confident and happy. "No it's not. Not completely. Have you made room in your life for the living planet?"

"Here they come," says the sister.

Ships Bend in. Dozens. A hundred. So many of them. All the big banks are there. Hosenfeffer – they're number two. An enormous carrier right next to us. I don't even owe them money. They came for Sara Foyle. Her name calls like the Devil.

Suddenly the room is full of sounds, clicks and notes. "The world feels threatened, and informs us of our imminent destruction," says the sister, translating. She sounds ecstatic about this too. Apparently a great compliment to have the talking planet threaten your life.

Amongst all the code, we start to hear human voices, transmissions from the Bank ships. They recite the legalities. They have all the time in the world. We can't escape. Sara brought us in so close. Embraced as we are in the planet's gravity, we can't Bend away.

Instead of defeat, Sara's face shows grim satisfaction. She planned this. I step over to a microphone and open a universal channel. "Get out of here, ladies and gents. This is something new. My god, get yourselves out of here."

One of the Bank captains offers an image. He appears mid-sentence, coldly lecturing on the violation of contract. But nothing indicates that he needs to die. He's a silver-haired man, in a beautiful Bank uniform. He's tying a cravat. Bravery in his jaw. On no notice, he's come hurtling across the universe to enforce the law.

"Captain," I plead. "Turn your ship out of the gravity. Do you see that world? Don't you see it?"

He actually does glance to his side. The sight must take his attention for a moment. Then he raises his chin as though to listen.

We're getting it too, a flurry of tones. Sara's sister translates. "The planet speaks. 'What is good man?' Any ship that can answer will be welcome. Yes. 'Who—is—good—man?'"

Sara laughs at the planet's choice. "'Goodness?' The perfect question for these leeches."

The image of the captain glances to me briefly then flickers out, his last words, "...kind of a big question, but I'll tell you, in my 22 years at the helm of a Bend carrier, I've..."

For us, Sara's sister answers. She answers and answers, without the planet acknowledging. Her mask ruins her human voice, but the answers are simple and beautiful. Human life has fixed value. We must share with each other. Least harm, most happiness...

"My god," I say. One of the Bank ships answered badly. Its seals open one by one as though a command passes through it by courier. Debris and bodies tumble out.

Sara nods with cold approval. "It wants the ships. Not the garbage." She's watching me.

Her sister sobs. Through the mask she says, "We too will be emptied." Her despair is the despair of a failed disciple. She has failed the test of her god, and she cries about that rather than our imminent destruction.

Another Bank ship vents. Bodies float. Cold and silent. Sara too – watching me cold and silent.

I say, "Your answers were fine. Is it a translation problem? What language?"

"No." The sister shakes her helmet sadly. "It's perfect universal protocol."

"Let me hear it."

"It's protocol. Anything you want to say I can translate back."

Sara nods to her sister, and we hear the sound. The planet

uses my voice. It asks, "Who is a good boy?" It repeats, "Who is a good boy?"

I clear my throat. "Banjo. Banjo is a good boy."

Notes sound in protocol. I look to the women. Beyond them, through the screen, is a fleet of empty shells. A hundred drifting ships. The clean lines of outer space are blurred, now, just as they are by the atmosphere on a living world. Here the dust is the floating crews. "I had a dog," I say. "Before. Banjo was his name. I had a dog when I was very very young."

# The Quarterly Review

## Reviews by Stephen Theaker, Jacob Edwards and Douglas J. Ogurek

---

### About Time
*Reviewed by Jacob Edwards*

*Rom-com, rom-chron or rom-con? Yorick to Defcon 3.*

Life beguiles us with many a misnomer, and one vital aspect of growing up is learning how to recognise and interpret these. Some are merely banal, such as the Australian parlance whereby redheads – like the protagonist of **About Time**, directed by Richard Curtis – may be referred to as Bluey. Others are more insidious. *Harlem Nights*, for instance, is billed as a black comedy (starring Eddie Murphy, Richard Pryor and Redd Foxx), yet is as humourless as a movie can be. *In Bruges* (Colin Farrell, Brendan Gleeson) adopts the same label and is just as dour, only with panther-pink lettering on its theatrical poster. Black comedy, like the gallows humour from which it was spawned, should make us laugh at something we wouldn't ordinarily find funny. Jihad satire *Four Lions* springs to mind as a rare instance where the appellation is fitting, but in a hopeless majority of cases only the good name of comedy is blackened; branded disingenuously so as to market something intrinsically lacking in *raison d'être*. Most genuinely black comedies (*Lock, Stock & Two Smoking Barrels*, for example, or *Seven Psychopaths*) steer well clear of the tag. Thus, any film actively promoting itself as a black comedy should be treated with the same distrust as a whole watermelon being flogged off on the cheap. What was it that Marcellus said to Horatio? Be wary of what you're buying into.

Sly though it is, black comedy remains relatively benign when compared to its big sister, the so-called *romantic* comedy, largest of the cinematic Billy Goats Bluff. True, the purveyors of black comedy might set out to short-change you, but it is romantic comedy that will scam you of your pension fund, or for just under half the population swindle you of your manhood. (And let's face it, Ray Davies singing about *Lola* is in many ways far more genuine an attempt at romantic comedy than whatever might be presented as such on the big screen.) Robert Sheckley's short story "A Ticket to Tranai" tells of a man who is lured to a wistfully described paradise planet, only to discover the dystopian truth behind its veneer and escape back to Earth, whereupon he settles down and out and begins telling to others the same misty-eyed tales that hooked him in the first place. Romantic comedies offer much the same experience. *Romance*, sigh the ladies. *Comedy*, shrug the men. Yet, even though neither is in evidence, escape from the carpet padded walls most often will culminate not in condemnation but rather in effusive (if somewhat mumbled and ashamed) spruiking of the silver screen paradise just fled. Romantic comedy, let it be said, is intrinsically a neither here nor there genre. Even Richard Curtis (*Blackadder*, *Mr Bean*), try though he might to have moved across to Feature Film Land without dipping his toes in gormless plot varnish or being sucked ever closer to the bathroom sink plughole of relationship dross and kneejerk hammered-home humour, has with *About Time* succumbed to an unconscionable measure of blandness.

Tim (Domhnall Gleeson) learns from his father (Bill Nighy) that he can travel in time anywhere within the span of his life to the present moment. The world now is Tim's oyster, but it proves lamentably squidgy with disappointment... until he meets Mary (Rachel McAdams) and romance contrives to go all *Sliding Doors* on him. The lead players are excellent but three pearls doth not a necklace make. Beyond the actors' delivery, some nice touches in dialogue and the film's distinct Britishness, is there really anything to set *About Time* apart from all the other runners who have stuffed themselves into romance/comedy horse-suits and galloped clumsily up to the box office? Watchable but uninspiring. It's a photo finish. And yet...

Tim's first thought when he learns of the family gift is – like everyone else's – that he might inside trade on reality and make himself a fortune. *No, you don't want to do that*, his dad warns him, although not on moralistic grounds or due to foreboding, Damoclean visions of a future turned sour. (After all, the family has watched movies together every Friday night of Tim's life. Somewhere along the line they must have seen *Back to the Future II*.) No, the danger of following the rainbow to its glittering end is that it's too easy. It would change Tim at some fundamental level; make him indolent; suck the marrow from his core identity. Benevolently casual, his father dismisses the thought. The pot of gold is just a reflexive wish, he suggests. It's like the default settings on Microsoft products, offering beneath its Midas-well illusion of happiness nothing more than a sure and certain abandonment of hope. In a more carcinogenic grilling this idea would be explored further, but as per the dictates of romantic comedy Tim takes his dad at his word and breezes on to his next thought for what to spend his gift on: finding a girlfriend.

At this point one might well expect something in the vein of *Groundhog Day*, where Phil Connors (Bill Murray), throughout the course(s) of a looped, purgatorial day, comes to know and serenade Rita (Andie MacDowell). But whereas Murray's character changed – or in his less scrupulous moments, at least *pretended* to change – quite profoundly in consequence of this pursuit, Gleeson's Tim stays very much in character and limits his temporal excursions to undoing moments where his own actions have given him cause to lament. Indeed, Tim meets and hits it off with Mary sans any recourse to the family gift. It is only after accidentally erasing this perfect first encounter that he has then to bring it about again through artificial, more comedically ineffectual means. *About Time* may present itself in familiar guise, but the cheesy trappings are spring-loaded and even the pseudo humorous stock characters *in extremis* (the caustic playwright, for example, or Tim's overly short-statured workmate) seem custom cut to compensate for a genre-anathematic lack of foibles in the lead characters. When Tim resists the clichéd impulse to sleep with his formerly unrequited first love, even though her invitation is one he could take up and then revise, there is more at play than Richard Curtis thumbing his nose at the rom-com rules of engagement. Not only does Tim show uncommon good sense in steering clear of such fallen plot lines, he actually takes inspiration from the danger thus avoided and so asks Mary to marry him. He resists the temptation to make his rained-out wedding more traditionally perfect. He embraces his father's wisdom of living each day twice and thus taking the time to appreciate the beauty of everyday life. In fact, by the end of the film Tim has advanced this concept to a new level, whereby he has no need of his innate ability to go CTRL + Z. If time travel has taught him anything, it is the redundancy of time travel. Life itself is the gift.

*About Time*, then, uses its titular hook not so much as a plot device but rather, through *disuse*, as a means by which to emphasise theme... and surprisingly there *is* a theme, hidden away but ready to be prised from within the clammed shut jaws of romance and comedy. Yes, there is romance. Yes, there is comedy. And yes, the trend set by *Four Weddings and a Funeral*, *Notting Hill* and *Love Actually* does with this continuation suggest a distinct preferential swing from the latter to the former. But at heart *About Time* is about family: Tim's mother, father, sister and uncle (the nucleus of his childhood); his girlfriend-then-wife, their children together (his adult family); and throughout, most tellingly, the father/son relationship that Gleeson and Nighy portray so winningly, and the way in which, over time, the son becomes himself a father and his outlook shifts from that of one who needs guidance to that of one who must provide it. When Tim's sister, Kit Kat, is injured in a car crash, Tim's immediate response is to go back and refashion her life for the better... until he discovers that this will change the identity of his own daughter. When his father dies, Tim still travels to the past to visit and seek his counsel... until such time as those trips would come to affect Tim's perception of his soon-to-be-born third child. In essence, the time travel aspects of *About Time* are put forward not to facilitate, but rather to put a constraint on, notions of omnipotence; and if the causality doesn't seem always to hold up – and despite much of the detail being glossed over, it really doesn't – then this is because the whys and wherefores have been painted in as no more than a backdrop to the more pivotal shift in Tim's parental perspective. *About Time* deserves recognition not under the accords of romantic run-around farce or uproarious misadventure, but rather for its gentle, heartfelt exploration of what truly it means to grow up and take on familial responsibilities; and in this respect Richard Curtis has succeeded admirably... even if he and his chosen genre fall paradoxically short of the expectations most viewers will have brought with them to the film.

---

## Computing with Quantum Cats: from Colossus to Qubits
*Reviewed by Jacob Edwards*

*Out of the bag, into the box seat.*

Few thought experiments have proved as alluring to scientific dilettantes (and not a few experts) as that of

Schrödinger's cat, which currently bestrides the podium of popular imagination sandwiched between the twin paradox and its more fanciful rival, the grandfather paradox. Intended as a *reductio ad absurdum*, the both dead and alive cat quickly took on a life far beyond what Schrödinger had intended. Now, 78 years since its callous (if purely conceptual) incarceration within quantum theory's diabolical box, the cat continues to exist as both misunderstood moggie and feline forerunner to the cult of Big Brother celebrity. Little wonder, then, that science writer John Gribbin in **Computing with Quantum Cats: from Colossus to Qubits** (Bantam Press, 296pp) has taken it in and positioned its milk bowl prominently on the cover of his book on quantum computers. When pitching to new readers, Schrödinger's cat may prove as iconic a lure as Dr Seuss's.

Quantum computers, Gribbin explains, will derive their mindboggling (but as yet unrealised) computational power by replacing conventional binary switches ("bits") with electrons, photons or single atoms that have been placed in a state of superposition to create "quantum bits" (in the vernacular, "qubits"). Unlike the classical forerunners of today, qubits are not limited to binary operations, and so will increase exponentially in processing power with every qubit added. Their superpositionary state should allow for an extraordinary variant of parallel processing, whereby different components of an operation are carried out, in essence, by variants of the same quantum computer operating concurrently across a multitude of parallel universes! *Forget the cat*, exclaim interested parties from big business and the military. Theoretically speaking (for now), a relatively early model quantum computer could, in just a few minutes, crack an RSA algorithmic code that would take a computer of today more time to break than the universe is old. But this, Gribbin assures us, has already gone well beyond theorists building castles in the air. This is cutting-edge development on the ground floor. It's gobsmacking, yes, but not just in the abstract sense. It's *happening*.

This makes for a compelling read once Gribbin follows up on his introductory remarks and starts delving into the potentials and pitfalls and the sheer ingeniousness of the work being carried out around the world in pursuit of quantum computing. Unfortunately, though, the breakthrough from theory to practice has left the field in a state of such rapid advancement that he is unable to keep up (not mentally, but in terms of publishing), and so Gribbin puts his book forward less as an examination of quantum computers *per se*, and more as a broad spectrum overview, in which he explores – through a series of biographical studies – the history, first of computers (Alan Turing, Johnny Von Neumann, et al.), then quantum theory (Richard Feynman, John Bell, etc.) and, only in the closing third of the book, the boxing together of one with the other (David Deutsch) and how we may expect them now to interact. Much of this subject matter is fascinating in its own right, and to his credit Gribbin does take pains to make the links explicit and place each scientific development in the future context of quantum computing. He also, however, does his material a mild disservice by periodically namedropping both himself and his earlier books (one of which inexplicably finds its way into the colour plates, sitting at once proudly yet pathetically beneath a rather more awe-inspiring group photo of physicists attending the Solvay Congress of 1927). Gribbin clearly knows what he's talking about, but this element of self-justification, taken alongside a list of previous publications and also his admission that quantum computing has not yet proven ready to settle down into an observable or measurable state, does rather give the impression of a career writer looking for but not quite finding a suitable topic for his next project.

Notwithstanding this apparent wave function collapse of *raison d'être*, John Gribbin demonstrates throughout *Computing with Quantum Cats* an assured grasp of his material, a manifest enthusiasm and – apropos of a discipline where Schrödinger must in some universe have described a panda bear, not a cat – the ability to cut through the bamboozlement and make accessible (without dumbing down or sending the curious layman into a stupor) concepts that otherwise would leave our heads locked in a quantum spin. The book's title may be misleading, but its content is engrossing – if not necessarily in expectant light of those quantum computers that in prototype form are factorising 15 and purring away in university and institute boxes as yet closed to us, then at least as a heads-shaking-in-wonderment, hats-in-the-air celebration of some of the finest scientific minds of the twentieth century (and beyond). *From Colossus to Qubits*, runs Gribbin's subtitle, and although "Colossus" here refers to the first electronic computer (of which ten were eventually made, prompted by advancements to Germany's Enigma code and used to break a vital Tunny transmission in the lead-up to D-Day), Gribbin might just as well have written "Colossi", in reference to the human giants whose collective intellect has paved the way from World War Two valves and plugboards to the ethereal qubits of today's computing battlefront. Regardless of your affinity (or otherwise) for the pressganged cat, theirs is a story well worth reading.

---

# Diablo III
*Reviewed by Stephen Theaker*

**Diablo III** (Blizzard Entertainment, Xbox 360; purchased) is the first of the series I've played, and since I don't play games on the PC, the Xbox 360 version is a new game to me. It's an isometric dungeon crawler, an action RPG where your heroes run around semi-randomly generated environments bashing hordes of creatures, fulfilling simple fetch-quests. Players can choose from wizard, demon hunter, barbarian, witch doctor and monk, and from male and female versions of each. The setting is pretty much indistinguishable from other fantasy games, with your regulation ghosts, zombies, skeletons etc to fight. Sometimes you get a funny feeling you're just playing *Dragon Age: Origins* or *Oblivion* from a different point of view, though some laser-like magical powers would be more at home in *Halo*.

It feels slightly odd to be enjoying the game so much (we've yet to stop playing it), since there's little here that wasn't present in much older console games like *Baldur's Gate: Dark Alliance*. This kind of gameplay more commonly shows up cut-price in the Xbox Live Arcade these days, in games like *Torchlight*, *Realms of Ancient War* and *Daggerdale*. The graphics, though they are pretty enough, don't feel at first like a ten-year advance on *Dark Alliance*. But as enemies, powers and enemies' powers accumulate you realise how well it all works, the game never visibly slowing despite the hundreds of objects flying around. The more you play, the more you appreciate the neat little touches that show how much work went into it.

It has a chemistry and balance that is difficult to define, though having a drop-in-drop-out four-player mode which works so well accounts for some of it. Put your controller down to sip your cup of tea and your character ambles along after your friends on their own – teleporting if need be – avoiding the most frustrating aspect of some previous games in a similar vein.

Similarly, a capacious sixty-slot backpack (at least in easy mode, in which we began playing it) makes for a free and easy approach to loot. As does the knowledge that it's all fairly random: in other role-playing games, you worry that failing to explore every tunnel in every location might mean missing out on your one chance in a fifty-hour playthrough to get a key piece of equipment. Here you can just run around dungeons aimlessly looking for fights, and then afterwards check the map for unexplored territory. And you can save at any time without losing any treasure, making it perfect for brief gaming sessions.

It's not very long, but like, say, the *Dynasty Warriors* games it's designed to be replayed over and over, your character levelling up, acquiring magical weapons and armour, and training their travelling artisans. What I would think of as the "proper" roleplaying elements are perfunctory, the dialogue skippable, non-branching and quite missable, it being unnecessary (at least so far as I have found to date) to talk to anyone other than the indicated characters to acquire quests. It's a vehicle stripped down to its chassis: fight monsters, open chest, get treasure, sell treasure. An endless torrent of glittering gold!

When I mention playing it with the children, you might look with concern to its age rating. But though it's rated 15 by the BBFC, the ratings board judges games via video recordings rather than playthroughs, and, aside from a few particularly gory dungeons which I had to face alone, I've found this to be a super game to play with the younglings: they just love throwing jars full of spiders at the bad guys. Mrs Theaker has been playing it regularly too, *despite* the jars full of spiders, and I'd say it's been our favourite family game since *Castle Crashers* and *Scott Pilgrim*.

The only flaw with regard to the multiplayer seems to be that all of us share one game save, regardless of who is logged in. It's a bit annoying to have to wipe out my progress on a level when the children want to log in and play a section that's a bit less challenging on a lower difficulty level. Maybe that's because everyone created their characters within my initial game save, but it's the only Xbox 360 game we've ever played that behaves in that way.

As usual, I haven't played the game online, so I can't comment on that. But otherwise, highly recommended, especially if you have chums at home to play it with.

---

## Doctor Who: The Day of the Doctor
*Reviewed by Jacob Edwards*

*John F. Who?*

When *Doctor Who* reached its tenth year of production – truly a remarkable feat – the programme celebrated with a special that brought together each of the Doctor's incarnations to that point, *The* (eponymous) *Three Doctors*. Objectively the story was quite weak, and William Hartnell's ill-health prevented him from making more than a token appearance, but the nostalgia element was priceless and the interaction between Patrick Troughton and Jon Pertwee nevertheless gave fans some *haute cuisine* over which to salivate.

Ten years later *Doctor Who* still was riding astonishingly high, and so came a twentieth anniversary special, *The Five Doctors*. Once more the show was padded heavily with nostalgia, and consequently suffered from there being too many characters (even after Tom Baker declined to take part, appearing only via archival footage; his Madame Tussaud's dummy was used for the publicity shoot). Viewers may have been treated to the memorable sight of a Raston Warrior Robot slicing up Cybermen, but this was the lone piece of originality. For the most part *The Five Doctors* was a carnival float turned pileup down memory lane, where again the most enjoyable sequences – lamentably sparse – come by way of the various Doctors interacting.

Fast forward another thirty years and the iconic blue police box finds itself spinning towards *Doctor Who*'s fiftieth anniversary. Mindboggling and momentous as this is, *ipso facto* it presents writer Steven Moffat with a number of problems. New Series *Doctor Who* comprises "only" nine of those fifty years, while the previous nine years saw no television *Who* at all, the TV movie remains an isolated stepping stone (preceded itself by a six year void), and the bulk of the programme's history looms large but inaccessibly distant in the form of *Doctor Who*'s original run from 1963 to 1989. Doctors one, two and three are deceased, as is the epoch-bridging companion, Sarah Jane Smith; Doctors four through seven are aging; Doctor eight (McGann) is castaway and largely forgotten on his island; Doctor nine – the fantastic first of the New Series tyros – cannot be persuaded to reprise his role. Effectively this leaves David Tennant and Matt Smith... and then countless companions, villains, monsters and audience expectations to sift through and mould together into a coherent story. Steven Moffat has written some tremendous *Doctor Who* episodes, and has shown with *Sherlock* that he can handle a feature length treatment. The fiftieth anniversary special, however, is in some ways the culmination of a patchwork story arc – one that spans half a century! – and with *The Wedding of River Song* Moffat equally showed that he can bring such an arc to the most muddled and scatterbrained of finales; a paean to extravagance. For all his knowledge and love of *Doctor Who*, how possibly can he make *The Day of the Doctor* work?

Or, to materialise back into a past tense perspective, how *did* he?

Firstly, by adopting a (mostly) sensible approach to Classic *Who*, paying homage to the early days but not allowing them in any significant way to feature. There is no K-9 or Katy Manning (despite their fairly recent appearances in *The Sarah Jane Adventures*); no Janet Fielding or Frazer Hines; and much though our nostalgia might clamour for one of the original Doctors to wind back the childhood clock, Moffat has recognised (quite rightly) that such wistful rubbing of the lamp is best reserved for vignettes such as the delightful charity special, *Time Crash* (2007). Tremendous though the early Doctors were, and even if somehow they could materialise without the rigours of time having rendered them dreadfully incongruous, the nature of the modern programme is such that their *characters* would not easily fit in. While Peter Davison's *The Five(ish) Doctors Reboot* acknowledges this in a playful yet telling coda, *The Day of the Doctor* brings back only the original opening titles sequence of 1963 and the shape-changing aliens from 1975's *Terror of the Zygons*. The choice of monster is particularly astute, spurning not only crossovers (Daleks, Cybermen, the Master, et cetera) but also new favourites such as the Weeping Angels, in favour of something that is distinctly old school. It's a significant nod, whereas everything else – notwithstanding some fleeting allusions – is new, albeit with the odd multi-coloured scarf left lying about the place.

Oh, and Tom Baker. Now, what the American panda bear was that about?? Continuity must not be allowed to constrain a programme so long-running as *Doctor Who*, and in fact when Matt Smith towards the end of the story starts ruminating about a life of retirement, the subsequent appearance of a much aged curator-cum-mothballed fourth Doctor (or some such) could just about be explained as this incarnation's having gone AWOL and fleetingly hung up the proverbial scarf sometime during 1980's *The Leisure Hive*; but really, what was the point? *The Day of the Doctor* already seems a tad cavalier in blockade-running the timey-wiminess of *Doctor Who*'s in-house science (vale the Blinovich Limitation), but at least that serves a narrative purpose. If Steven Moffat was looking for a cameo from bygone days, a much more apposite choice would have been founding cast member William Russell, whose character is noted in passing as being now chairman of the governors at Coal Hill School. Ah, well. Moving on.

Moffat's second piece of perspicacity was to streamline the New Series content – no Jack Harkness, Martha or Donna, Rory or Amy – and instead afford as much screen time as practicable to interactions between incumbent Matt Smith and his predecessor David Tennant. As with *The Three Doctors* and *The Five Doctors*, this interplay is very much the highlight, and here it has been more deliberately and substantially scripted. Furthermore, Moffat gives the two expected Doctors a third, new-but-old Doctor against whom to play. Setting *The Day of the Doctor* partly in the canonical void between Classic and New Series *Who*, rather than as a freestanding story, seems at once fitting yet overly ambitious; bold but fraught with impertinence; and even with pre-emptive misgivings put aside, truth be told it does still seem a little odd to have cast John Hurt as a Valeyard-esque pseudo-incarnation of the Doctor from somewhere between two incarnations. (Indeed, rather than having Paul McGann's eighth Doctor regenerate into this so-called War Doctor – in *The Night of the Doctor*, a mini-episode prefix that many viewers won't have seen – why did Moffat not simply feature McGann throughout?) Yet, the effect is arresting, and must count as a triumph in respectfully pitting New Series *Who* against a newly minted representation of the Classic serial.

This, of course, makes the Tom Baker inclusion even more bewildering; but again, moving on...

*The Day of the Doctor* is not perfect – how could it be? – and there remains an odd disparity in Moffat's having run intertwined plot lines, one of which (the Zygons) is treated quite convivially while the other (the Time War) is rendered with almost epic pathos. Both strands skirt close to excess. Frivolity and magniloquence lie frayed at the edges. But perhaps this in some measure is necessary. *Doctor Who* has been many things over the years, and those who scrutinise it too much are in danger, surely, of missing the point. Yes, David Tennant might soliloquise to a floppy-eared bunny, but his babbling is a veneer – consciously recognised – that covers his background processing; and if the three Doctors show a dazzling, egoistic exuberance in jointly outwitting what transpires to be an unlocked door, then this too is only a mask worn in contrast to the doubt and insecurity to which John Hurt falls prey at his lowest ebb. The magic wand that has sustained *Doctor Who* across fifty years is the yin of the Doctor's vulnerability swirled ever around the yang of omnipotence. Little wonder, then, that Steven Moffat chose to emphasise these characteristics, and little wonder the incantation once again succeeded in conjuring an appreciative audience.

Fifty years to the day since William Hartnell made his slightly muted debut in black and white on the transitory cathode ray tubes of British television – or to put it another way, fifty years and a day since JFK was assassinated – Matt Smith and Company now have lofted the torch in a pyrotechnic celebration simulcast to TV and cinema screens across ninety-four countries. For all the hype, this so easily could have resulted in a great let-down; but thankfully not. The milestone has been celebrated. We've had our day with the Doctor(s). All around the world glasses were clinked, and nobody was hurt. All told, not too bad. Now, on with the show...

---

# Doctor Who: The Light at the End
*Reviewed by Stephen Theaker*

**Doctor Who: The Light at the End**, by Nicholas Briggs (Big Finish, digital audio, 2 hrs; purchased from publisher) gives us the impossible dream: a team-up of Doctors four (Tom Baker), five (Peter Davison), six (Colin Baker), seven (Sylvester McCoy) and eight (Paul McGann) in their prime, accompanied respectively by companions Leela (Louise Jameson), Nyssa (Sarah Sutton), Peri (Nicola Bryant), Ace (Sophie Aldred) and Charley (India Fisher). That's not to mention cameos from Sara Kingdom, the first three Doctors (somehow!), Jamie, Zoe, Tegan, Turlough and I'm sure many others that I missed on a first listen. With all those people involved, does the story matter? You get to hear the fourth Doctor talking to the eighth Doctor! Who cares what they're talking about?

Well, just in case you do: five of the Doctors (or their companions) notice flashing red lights on their consoles. The problem is not just the flashing, but that the lights have never been there before: they seem to have been created and set off by the Tardis passing through a specific location on November 23rd, 1963. So off the Doctors go to investigate. It's a bit like a Justice League of America story from the sixties, as four and eight team up, and six and seven, while five has to fend for himself, before they all gather together for the big finale. Since he's on the cover, it's no spoiler to say that the Master is involved.

He's played with a nice subtlety by Geoffrey Beevers, who

played the decayed Master in "The Keeper of Traken" (that version having been first portrayed by Peter Pratt in "The Deadly Assassin"). I think it used to be generally assumed that the decayed Master was the Roger Delgado incarnation at the end of his life, but here he seems in *slightly* better condition – he's described by an unfortunate human who encounters him as looking like he's been "injured, burnt" – and on the cover he looks recognisably like Geoffrey Beevers, which would seem to establish him as an entirely separate incarnation from Delgado (if he hadn't been already).

The story does show the difficulty of a story involving so many of the Doctors and their companions, in that there isn't much time for anything else. I came away from it with a renewed appreciation of the television story "The Five Doctors", always one of my favourites. Terrance Dicks did a brilliant job there of giving all four Doctors a moment to shine, and gave each of them memorable, quotable dialogue. In *The Light at the End*, Nicholas Briggs has five fully active Doctors, plus quite big cameos from three more, and so even two hours doesn't allow time for many other speaking roles. Like Dicks with his walks to the tower, Briggs keeps things quite simple, focusing on one really sticky problem, allowing his Doctors time to talk around it.

It's interesting that here, as in many recent television stories, the biggest danger is not that the Doctor might die, but that he might never have existed: as he approaches his regeneration limit, his past becomes more important than his future. As in previous anniversary stories, we once again see the later Doctors defer to the first – odd when the eighth Doctor is about four times older! Perhaps it's because he's the only one with direct memories of the Time Lord academy, while all the rest have had their youthful memories jumbled by multiple regenerations.

The absence of the tenth Doctor is a shame, given that David Tennant was working on Big Finish audios long before he took the Tardis keys, but better a contract that lets

Big Finish only make stories with the classic Doctors than no contract to make new stories at all. And it's right that Big Finish's celebration of the programme's fiftieth anniversary should celebrate the Doctors and companions with whom they've had so many terrific adventures. Caroline Johns, Mary Tamm, Nicholas Courtney and Elisabeth Sladen are of course missed even more, but well done Big Finish for giving us so many new stories with them while it was still possible.

This is everything I thought I wanted from the television anniversary episode, but didn't expect to get. As many Doctors as possible, on one adventure, interacting with each other: I won't deny that happy tears were emitted! It gave me that crossover rush without ever becoming a panto. Though it was with a mere three Doctors for the most part, Steven Moffat gave us something special in his anniversary special, and this story did a marvellous job of clearing the decks in preparation, leaving this listener ready for whatever November 23rd, 2013 had in store, fannish cravings sated. And maybe at some point there was a flashing red light on the Doctors' consoles in "The Day of the Doctor" and I just didn't notice it. An absolute must-buy for any Doctor Who fan.

---

## Doctor Who and the Pescatons
*Reviewed by Stephen Theaker*

It has been quite a while since I last dipped into the six-story collection *Doctor Who: The BBC Radio Episodes*. I began with the Jon Pertwee story *The Paradise of Death*, reviewed in these pages many years ago, and it wasn't too bad. A bit later I listened to *The Ghosts of N-Space*, which was so painfully awful I couldn't bring myself to review it, especially since that was shortly after the deaths of Elisabeth Sladen and Nicholas Courtney and it wasn't the right time to give their work a slating, however richly deserved. If you haven't heard that story and you're curious what was so bad about it, as an example let's just say I never needed to hear the third Doctor explain the meaning of "sodomite" to Sarah Jane Smith.

Recently I've found that the new Audible iPad app is a very nice way to listen to audiobooks, and it's kind enough to let you listen to non-Audible titles too, so I've been digitising and loading onto the iPad a lot of older audio adventures that got lost in the rush originally. Where those are ones I bought (for example the first eight in the Big Finish Companion Chronicles series, picked up in a sale), I may or may not review them, depending on whether I have time, but where (like this story) they were originally submitted for review and got stuck in the pile I will try to do the honours, though it's a couple of years late. I don't suppose anyone comes to this magazine expecting timely reviews.

So, explanations aside, on to a short review of **Doctor Who and the Pescatons** (AudioGO, 1×CD, 46 mins; supplied by publisher), which was (the box says) originally broadcast on BBC Radio on 27 August 1993, but first existed as an LP in the seventies. This again features Elisabeth Sladen as Sarah Jane, this time paired with Tom Baker as the fourth Doctor, making this a rare example of a spin-off featuring the current on-screen cast. It's really more of a story told by the Doctor than a drama. Sarah Jane's contributions are very limited, and the only other speaking part is Zor (Bill Mitchell), the leader of the baddies who pops up for a couple of scenes. The script is by Victor Pemberton, who had previously written the seaweed serial "Fury from the Deep".

The plot concerns, you won't be surprised to learn, the Pescatons, who are a shark-like species of aliens who can walk around on land using their flippers. Though their invasion of Earth is motivated by the need to escape their own doomed planet, there are few shades of grey here: the Doctor says this is a clash between two civilisations, one good (by which I think he means us), one evil (probably the Pescatons). The invasion leads to some terrifying sequences where Pescatons wander round London eating people up.

The screams are so full-blooded you worry for the sanity of any children who got their hands on the LP! But I wish *I* had.

Looked at objectively, this story isn't terribly good, but it is a great deal of fun and a fascinating product of its time. Given its short length I'm sure this won't be the last time I listen to it. It's just a shame that there are no songs! A fan of Jeff Wayne's *War of the Worlds* can't help hearing the points in this story at which a disco beat might reasonably have kicked in, leading us off to new worlds of groovy Whovian fun. Justin Heywood singing for the Doctor, Sarah Brightman for Sarah Jane, David Essex for the Pescaton leader. It would have been glorious! But you can't have everything. Someone should really get Tom Baker involved in a project like that: his brief contribution to Mansun's *Six* shows how magnificent it could be.

---

## Doctor Who and the Planet of the Daleks
*Reviewed by Stephen Theaker*

I've lost track of how often I've read the Target edition of **Doctor Who and the Planet of the Daleks** (AudioGO, digital audiobook, 3 hrs 3 mins; Audible purchase) by Terrance Dicks, but as soon as I saw this reading by Mark Gatiss (with Dalek voices by Nicholas Briggs) it attracted the attention of my monthly Audible token. That voice! Imagine him reading this: "The cover illustration of this book portrays the third Doctor Who, whose physical appearance was altered by the Time Lords when they banished him to the planet Earth in the twentieth century." In the first story of his fourth season, the third Doctor (with the help of his earlier selves) had won back the right to travel in time and space, but as usual flew straight into serious trouble. First came the drashigs, and then the incipient space war between the human and Draconian empires, a war engineered by the dastardly Daleks to pave the way for their invasion. This story begins with Jo Grant watching over the injured Doctor, the Tardis being sent by the Time

Lords to Spiridon. She'll soon venture out for help, and end up in the hands of its invisible inhabitants, but as the title suggests, this is no longer their planet. The Doctor will eventually wake and go looking for Jo, only to meet a squad of Thals, here to destroy a Dalek base at any cost.

The original television episodes were written by Terry Nation in 1973, ten years after he first introduced the Daleks. The story is in many ways a throwback to those earlier episodes. The Tardis is incapacitated, the companion falls ill and will die if not treated, the Thals are attacking a Dalek base, there is a lot of running around in jungles. The third Doctor is as dismissive of others as the first Doctor ever was: reunited with Jo after she's been crawling around the Dalek base, he doesn't let her speak, because there's no way she could *possibly* have any important information for him. And the Tardis interior is so tiny that the Doctor exhausts its air in a matter of hours after the exterior is smothered by Spiridon's plant life. Makes you wonder how its occupants survive when it is flying through space!

But despite its flaws, there has always been something magical about this story for me: it's *Where Eagles Dare* starring Doctor Who! Even now it seems unusual in being a sequel to a story from two Doctors before. And like many of the Pertwee-era stories, it benefits greatly from the Target novelisation: ironically, stories that were rather too long on television become quick-paced, action-packed adventures when compressed down to little over a hundred pages. This is a typical example, its three hours gripping in precisely the way that the six television episodes were not.

The audiobook includes fun sound effects and music stings, and Mark Gatiss's narration is perfect, an absolute delight. Unless my memory is playing tricks, I once had a cassette copy of Jon Pertwee's reading of the same book, and it surprises me to say I prefer this version. It's unabridged, so that helps, but it always seemed odd to have the Doctor reading a text in which he was a character. As read by Gatiss, even the worst dialogue of the story ("I'm qualified in space medicine, I'll do what I can for your friend") becomes something to savour, and he tickles the listener with those words and phrases which adults may find amusing (the noise made by the plants splatting on the Tardis). However many times you've read the book or watched the episodes, this audio version is well worth a listen.

# Gravity

*Reviewed by Jacob Edwards*

*Seeds in orbit – the apple of Newton's Imax.*

Mission specialist and first-time astronaut Ryan Stone (Sandra Bullock), accompanied by garrulous veteran Matt Kowalski (George Clooney), is servicing the Hubble Space Telescope when debris from a Russian satellite sets off a chain reaction that severely damages their spaceship, leaving Stone and Kowalski adrift and with only ninety minutes before the gathering cloud of debris completes a planetary orbit and sweeps past them again. Cut off from Mission Control, their only hope is to use Kowalski's MMU (Manned Manoeuvring Unit) to traverse the hundred kilometres between them and the International Space Station.

Irish poet Johnny Byrne, who in 1975 script-edited the first season of cult British SF series *Space: 1999*, later in life said that, "Pace is not just fast movement. Pace is the way in which character relationships are unravelling, and that can happen in absolutely static situations."[1] Whether or not this maxim stemmed in some measure from the technical limitations of television (and film) production in Byrne's time, palpably it is wisdom that few modern-day Hollywood filmmakers have deigned to take on board. Blockbusters in particular tend to choke on their own action, vomiting out so-called plot until the cinema screen is smeared with an implausible, off-coloured and above all pointless choreography of two-left-footed movements executed purely for the sake of movement. There are some notable exceptions, of course, but when American studios table a Thanksgiving budget of $100 million, the result usually is not *haute cuisine* so much as a big fat turkey ready for basting. Even in Hollywood, however, not everything is Yankee Doodle Dandy.

Apart from its moneybag-toting distributor (Warner Bros) and smallest-possible-ensemble cast (in essence just Bullock and Clooney, backed briefly by the voice of Ed Harris), *Gravity* shows precious little allegiance to the stars and stripes. Perhaps this is coincidental, but under the direction of Mexican virtuoso Alfonso Cuarón (*Children of Men*), aided by his compatriot, cinematographer Emmanuel Lubezki (*The Tree of Life*) and co-produced respectively by British and Mexican companies Heyday Films (*Harry Potter 1–8*) and Esperanto Filmoj (*Pan's Labyrinth*), *Gravity* presents as a movie not only with deep pockets but also the production values of a stilt-walker, thereby constituting one of those rare instances where the untold millions, rather than manifesting in flashing $$ signs on the bulging eyes of some Yosemite Sam film mogul in caricature, lusting after a dirty weekend with the box-office, instead have been spent on the proper and judicious pursuit of something genuinely mouth-watering. James Cameron (admittedly a friend of Cuarón's) has gone so far as to dub it "the best space film ever done", praising Bullock's performance, state of the art photography and, beyond the obvious achievement of having brought bleeding edge technology successfully to bear, Cuarón's exceptional pursuit and retention of creative control in an industry that habitually stamps out purity of vision.[2] Cuarón not only directed but also co-produced, co-wrote and (most unusually) co-edited the film, his overarching gubernatorial presence allowing for several cinematic ingredients that nowadays aren't staples of Tinseltown; most obviously, the prominence of the female lead (Bullock soon relegating Clooney to a supporting role), but also an assured, at times almost languorous pacing that deliberately contrasts the movie's action scenes against precisely the sort of static-yet-unravelling situations to which Johnny Byrne made reference. One aspect of this is Cuarón's favouring of single, long-sequence shots over the more Hollywood-standard frenetic slather of cutaways; and as tension and adrenaline mix and each reprieve segues achingly back into crisis, an emotionally fraught audience cannot help but feel the telling wisdom of shooting a thriller that periodically gives itself space in which to drift.

*Gravity* is visually stunning even in 2D, and though it takes the occasional liberty with physics (detaching teardrops in zero-G, for instance), it also has garnered praise from *bona fide* NASA astronauts such as Mike Massimino (who in 2009 carried out repairs to the Hubble Telescope)[3] and Scott Parazynski.[4] Accuracy is one thing – and it doesn't take too much frown to counterthrust a raised eyebrow at Clooney's untethering himself from Bullock – but in the case of *Gravity* (unlike the gung-ho shitstorm that Hollywood has left flying shrapnel-like across big screens around the world) it seems that Cuarón genuinely strived for realism, and that where this is lacking it is not through neglect or dumbing down but rather a deliberate, almost tenderly embraced necessity that he, like a bushman apologising to the animal he is about to kill, bowed to in order to feed the story. Or is that really the case? Before Cuarón can be recognised for his good intentions in this respect, first he must carry the can for what appear to be some rather less seemly employments of the dicta/directorial megaphone; for example, the blaring and overtly orchestrated crescendo-to-silence moments (which are too condescending to be effective) and sundry other fiddles that play more to fraudulent manipulation than any charitable enhancement of the audience's emotions. In 2010, for a fiftieth of the cost of *Gravity*, Spanish director Rodrigo Cortés gave us *Buried*, a one-man film depicting the harrowing phone conversations of an American who's been kidnapped in Iraq and wakes up buried alive with just his BlackBerry for company. *Gravity* transplants that claustrophobic panic onto the vast backdrop of space, but while the setting couldn't be more different, the effect – and in particular the level of contrivance necessary to concoct and then sustain such a volatile mix of hope and abandonment – is largely the same; and whereas *Buried* at least had the good grace to follow through on its promise, *Gravity* (despite one devilish curtain call by Clooney) in the end is rather shameless in bringing about the dénouement that is intended so poignantly to highlight the eponymous gravity now shown to have been absent all along... yes, it might leave one breathless, but it's also something of a debasement; like having the queen appear in full ceremonial pomp, only suddenly to break the fourth wall and start geeing up the crowd, motioning with both hands for them to send her victorious.

Critics to date have greeted *Gravity* with open arms – and rightly so, for in trading Hollywood's old beans for the more sangfroid cow of his own convictions, Cuarón shucks the prescribed idiocy of building castles in the air, and instead (a little counter-intuitively, maybe) brings us crashing down to Earth with heart-pounding reference not to magical beanstalks but rather the actual and present dangers of the real world. Which isn't to say that he's entirely scrupulous, or won't stoop occasionally to milking his audience, but there remains at heart a certain fidelity to Cuarón's filmmaking; a point-of-view immediacy through which *Gravity* outpaces the usual hyperbole in sweeping up viewers and barrelling them along. High opinions being well and truly susceptible to orbital decay (and in this instance re-entry seems inevitable), one wonders whether *Gravity* can possibly live up to its initial plaudits. Does it have either the re-watch value or sufficient complexity to be looked back on in future years as a classic? Perhaps not, but even if what people are gawping at today turns out to be something of a flash in the pan, undeniably it's a spectacle well worth checking out here and now amidst that first great rush on the silver screen.

1. Byrne, Johnny, *Doctor Who: The Keeper of Traken*, DVD Audio Commentary (BBC, 2007), 42:57–43:08.
2. Cohen, David S., and Dave McNary, "Alfonso Cuaron Returns to the Bigscreen After Seven Years With 'Gravity'", *Variety*, posted September 3, 2013 [http://variety.com/2013/film/news/alfonso-cuaron-returns-to-the-bigscreen-after-seven-years-with-gravity-1200596518/]
3. Azriel, Merryl, "Gravity: Ripped from the Headlines?", *Space Safety Magazine*, posted October 4, 2013 [http://www.spacesafetymagazine.com/2013/10/04/gravity-ripped-headlines/]
4. Watkins, Gwynne, "An Astronaut Fact-checks *Gravity*", *Vulture*, posted October 8, 2013 [http://www.vulture.com/2013/10/astronaut-fact-checks-gravity.html]

# Hatchet Job

*Reviewed by Stephen Theaker*

In **Hatchet Job** (Picador, digital audiobook, 7 hrs 53 mins; Audible purchase) Mark Kermode, perhaps the UK's most well-known film critic and certainly one of its most respected, covers all the big issues involved in writing reviews: being honest and only saying things you actually believe, trying to get the facts right, writing well, being entertaining, and, sometimes, changing your mind. He talks about the review as an art form in itself, and speaks scathingly of the idea that the only critics of any worth are those hoping to become film-makers. Kevin Smith, who espoused that view and, for example, cancelled the screenings of *Red State* for UK critics at the last minute, comes in for a great deal of criticism, as does Harry Knowles of Ain't It Cool News, for his habit of publishing any old nonsense that his readers might find interesting, whatever its source, and his practice of publishing anonymous reviews of unfinished films.

A big concern for Kermode is what gives a review weight.

Not just the words, but the person, publication and reputations standing behind them. He's hardly the kind of fuddy-duddy who says all online writing is a worthless, mindless babble – as he explains, everyone writes online now, and he has lots of kind things to say about online sites who have what he believes is a credible ethos, such as Film Threat. But he argues persuasively that a paid, named reviewer puts their reputation and livelihood on the line with every review, as does the publication that chooses to publish it, giving it an innate credibility that cannot be matched by an anonymous piece on Amazon.

A key phrase in the book is: "Opinions are ephemeral, but professional conduct is sacrosanct." Kermode tells a story about a falling-out with a distributor, thinking it was because he slated their film, only to realise it was because he'd implied that they hadn't even tried to market it. It would be depressing to hear Kermode talk about Richard Bacon and Johnny Vaughan's allegedly unethical approach to film reviewing if he didn't tell the stories in such a funny way. Bacon didn't watch the films he reviewed. That's bad enough. But in fact, he wasn't writing the reviews either, and hadn't even read them!

Sock-puppeteers in the book world like Stephen Leather and R.J. Ellory also attract his withering gaze, though not all bad behaviour comes in for such criticism: he seems overly forgiving of hero Ken Russell's bashing Alexander Walker over the head with a copy of his own review (or at least a rolled-up copy of the newspaper containing it). I think he takes an aggressive response to reviews almost as par for the course, having experienced similar things himself. As he explains: "many of the people who you most admire don't see much point in what you're doing". If Ken Russell had attacked Walker's integrity – as Kermode once did himself, something he now regrets – that would have been a different matter.

Kermode reads the audiobook himself, which of course enhances it immeasurably, making it a first-rate bonus feature to the Kermode and Mayo film show, though at first it takes some getting used to: he's speaking so slowly and carefully! There are some points at which, endearingly, and I think probably self-consciously (their careers do after all have certain parallels, except that Kermode hasn't cocked up his opportunities at the BBC), Kermode strays into Alan Partridge territory (don't we all?). A mention of the "information superhighway". "You've remembered it wrong. You've remembered it wrong. You've remembered it wrong. But I hadn't." Chapter 6's morning routine: "Monday morning. Alarm. Up. Wash. Let the dog out. Dog doesn't want to go out. Insist dog goes out. Dog not going out. Dog goes and lies on the sofa."

Those were some of my favourite moments, and the audiobook reminded me of Alan in another way, in that like *I, Partridge*, once I began listening to *Hatchet Job* I didn't stop, going through the whole thing in a couple of days. It's funny, moving and angry, all in the right places at the right time. Kermode knows what goes where, and why. It is recommended to every novice reviewer, and even old hands may find it useful. The book gets a bit soppy towards the end, as Kermode relates first the joy of seeing a childhood favourite again (*Jeremy*) and then his surrender to *A.I. Artificial Intelligence* (a film I watched with my fist in my mouth to stop myself bawling), followed by his awkward apology to Steven Spielberg for having got it wrong. So it's a relief at the end to hear him say, partly in response to news of a new Michael Bay Transformers film, "Where the hell did I leave that hatchet?"

---

# The Hunger Games: Catching Fire
*Reviewed by Douglas J. Ogurek*

*Rarely does a movie outshine the book that inspired it. The Hunger Games: Catching Fire blazes as an exception.*

*Catching Fire*, the middle instalment in Suzanne Collins's hugely popular Hunger Games trilogy, divides into two stories that could stand alone. The second and far better half details the Hunger Games' 75th anniversary "Quarter Quell". District 12 tributes (i.e. competitors) and winners of the last game, Katniss Everdeen and Peeta Mellark, square off in a fight-to-the-death match against past victors from the nation of Panem's other eleven districts. Collins writes about this battle royal with skill, and the film follows suit.

The first half of the novel, however, only fizzles in Katniss's introspection – the first person present narration doesn't help – about goings on within the districts, about the threats her sister and mother face, and about the two young men (Peeta and Gail) vying for her attention. It just takes too long to get to the good stuff.

This film version presents the two stories, but in the first half, it glides over the novel's boring elements, dispatches with the introspection, and moves quickly in and out of less emotionally charged scenes. Additionally, the diversity in settings, ranging from the cold and desolate Victors' Village where past Hunger Games winners reside to the technological pomposity and vivacious fashions at President Snow's Capitol party, brings to the film a visual interest that the novel cannot achieve.

The first half of the film chronicles Katniss and Peeta's victory tour, and drops hints, some subtle, others not so, at the rising tension between the wealthy Capitol and the twelve districts it oppresses. Katniss has her work cut out for her: she must keep her family safe from President Snow's threats by convincing Panem that she loves Peeta (despite her uncertainty); she must placate the districts whose children were slaughtered in the game that she and Peeta won; and she must come to terms with the districts' growing desire to embrace her as a symbol of revolution. All that, plus President Snow, the most powerful man in Panem, wants her dead.

The film shrewdly portrays the unrest within Panem. It's in the crowds that Katniss and Peeta address. It's in the graffiti that they glimpse while on the tour train, and it's in their reactions to the growing presence of Capitol soldiers.

As it transitions into the second half, the film transfers to the filmgoer the pre-game jitters as effectively as did its predecessor. Then there is the tension and disorientation when Katniss gets conveyed to the arena where the game takes place. Water. Sunlight. Trees. Other tributes. The camera pans. Where's Peeta? So much to absorb before the whistle blows and the killing begins.

New director Francis Lawrence takes a slightly different approach to showing the game. This time around, the most antagonistic players take a back seat to the dangers that the elaborate setting hurls at Katniss, Peeta, and their alleged allies. With fewer subplot cuts, the film more thoroughly immerses the viewer in the action. And when a character dies, it's fast. No dying speeches. No prolonged agony.

The film transcends other recent big budget action films by showing secondary characters with eccentricities and psychological, rather than physical, weaknesses. We meet individuals with backstories, and characters propelled by passions ranging from love to rage. Johanna Mason, portrayed as an axe-wielding femme fatale, strips naked in an elevator as her audience looks on with annoyance (Katniss), discomfort (Peeta), and admiration (drunken mentor Haymitch). *Catching Fire* also introduces District 4 playboy Finnick Odair. Although the flashy name underscores his arrogant façade, Odair is much more than a handsome hotshot.

A who's who of recent Oscar winners and nominees bolsters the *Catching Fire* cast. Philip Seymour Hoffman offers a subdued, but by no means sub par performance as head gamekeeper Plutarch Heavensbee. Unlike other Capitol minions, Heavensbee wears little makeup and avoids flamboyant clothes. His smirk and his calculated comments suggest that he knows something that other characters don't.

On the other extreme, actor Stanley Tucci endows

Hunger Games host Caesar Flickerman with a trademark cackle and a kind of disingenuous fascination with the tributes he interviews. Flickerman's gleaming teeth and purple hair are as vibrant as his movements and verbal flourishes. He is bullshit embodied.

Jennifer Lawrence's portrayal of Katniss Everdeen is convincing and emotionally engaging. When Katniss and Peeta address a silent District 11 crowd during their victory tour, families mourn beneath giant screens that show recorded footage of their fallen children. While Peeta speaks, Lawrence uses facial expressions to convey a complex mix of emotions.

The role of Katniss Everdeen in the contemporary motion picture canon deserves mention. The typical action film portrays women as one-dimensional, highly sexual objects. Katniss makes a refreshing departure. She doesn't use sexuality to get what she wants, nor does she rely on magic or super powers. She only has her intelligence, her resolve, and her drive to protect those she loves. Perhaps Katniss represents not only a redeemer to the people of Panem, but also a new kind of heroine to the filmgoing public. Things are catching fire indeed.

---

## Insufferable: The Complete First Season
*Reviewed by Stephen Theaker*

**Insufferable: The Complete First Season** (Thrillbent, ebook, 557pp; Comixology purchase) is written by Mark Waid, a writer whose work I've always liked, but who to my mind has stepped up a level of late, with art by Peter Krause, the two of them co-creating the series. It tells the story of a superhero and his sidekick, who fell out a couple of years ago: Nocturnus and Galahad. Think Batman and Robin, round about the time Dick Grayson got into a snit, dropped the cape and became Nightwing. Now imagine if Dick had revealed Batman's secret identity on live television. And in response Bruce had burned down Wayne Manor and gone into hiding while Dick became a celebrity idiot obsessed with fame and money. Then imagine Bruce and Dick were... well, no spoilers. Two years later, old enemies are returning to the fray and the dysfunctional duo are pushed back into collaboration, despite all the resentments.

This is a slightly unusual publication, in that you shouldn't expect a five hundred and fifty-seven page book, despite the page count. Firstly, each of these pages is the equivalent of a half-page in a regular comic, ideal for reading on a tablet in landscape mode, but there are frequently just two or three panels per page. Secondly, many pages feature the same art, with dialogue and colouring changing, or missing panels being filled in. In regular print format, this would perhaps be a hundred or so pages long. Also, many pages are given over to behind the scenes information: for example, the feud between Nocturnus and Galahad was apparently inspired by a pair of comic creators who fell out. (Grant Morrison and Mark Millar, maybe?)

But so long as you know all of that before purchasing, that you are not getting here the same amount of story that appeared in, for example, the *Irredeemable* omnibuses from the same creators, none of it is a problem; especially since it is priced accordingly. (And in fact the entire series is also available to read for free on the Thrillbent website.) There's obviously a sense that the art is being eked out, but it's fun to see the imaginative ways that comics are being reinvented on tablets, the new techniques being developed before our eyes. (Alex de Campi's *Valentine* is another innovator in this area.) Shadows being removed to reveal a second hostage, angry tweets popping up over the screen to barrage Galahad, Nocturnus suddenly appearing in a doorway: it's all very cleverly done.

The story is perhaps not yet quite as interesting as the techniques being used to tell it, but there are as many twists and revelations as you might expect. The returning supervillains don't make much of an impression, aside from one inventive showdown in a maternity ward. There's a big strong guy, another with sharp teeth, a serial slasher, and an assassin, but they're all just bit players in the family drama. The most intriguing villain introduced was (I thought) The Headmaster – a great name for a supervillain! – but unfortunately he turned out to be an actual headmaster, albeit not a very good one.

However, the strained relationship between Galahad and Nocturnus is totally convincing, and that's the heart of the story. Both have valid reasons for feeling the way they do, they've both made mistakes, and you spend the story rooting for them to sort it out. *Insufferable* isn't quite as good yet as *Irredeemable* or *Incorruptible*, but I read those from start to finish in one or two goes, and this story is only just beginning. It's a good superhero book told with innovative techniques, perfectly tailored for reading on your tablet.

---

## Journey into Space: The World in Peril
*Reviewed by Stephen Theaker*

**Journey into Space: The World in Peril** (BBC Audio, digital audiobook, 10 hours; Audible purchase), written by Charles Chilton, is the third story in the saga of Jet Morgan and his crew, following on from *Operation Luna* and *The Red Planet*, both of which I adored. The CD release of this conclusion passed me by, so it was an utter delight to discover it on Audible.

The twenty-episode story begins with Jet (captain), Mitch (the engineer), Lemmy (the radio operator) and Doc (have a guess) arriving back on Earth after their disastrous Martian mission, with news of a possible Martian invasion. Put into seclusion to keep Martian agents from knowing they survived, and to prevent a panic, the boys kick their heels until a new mission comes their way: to go back to Mars. A fine reward!

Earth wants them to gather more information about the invasion, and, ideally, capture a Martian or one of the conditioned humans who serve them. The mission becomes urgent when strange planetoids appear in Earth's orbit, and so after a brief sojourn on Luna while the ships are prepared it's back to Mars for our heroes.

This is that rarest of treasures, the third in a trilogy that lives up to parts one and two. One of the true joys of *Journey into Space* is that it's about characters who think very carefully. They chew everything over, consider every aspect and consequence of their decisions, argue intelligently with each other and their enemies, and are put into situations where careful thought is absolutely required and there's plenty of time to do it. I envy the people who got to listen to this series when it first came out, though waiting a week between episodes must have been quite trying: every episode brings an exciting revelation, a brilliant set-piece or a deadly cliffhanger.

One particular tour de force is the episode in which, after an attack on Mars, Lemmy wakes up in absolute darkness, and must step by step work out where he is, why the ceiling is so low, why his feet can't find any solid ground, if the rest of the crew are there too – and who the hell is that walking around the room with ice cold skin!

It's hard to imagine I could have enjoyed this series more, but it does have one failing: the lack of female characters. That, the class relationships and the assumption that listeners will pay attention are the only things that date it. The journey into space is a very long one, but it's highly rewarding, with an unexpected, perfect conclusion. Good work, Jet boy! (As Lemmy might say.)

# The Last Revelation of Gla'aki

*Reviewed by Stephen Theaker*

Leonard Fairman is an archivist at Brichester University, whose unwise curiosity regarding a series of occult volumes leads to his involvement in the events described by Ramsey Campbell in **The Last Revelation of Gla'aki** (PS Publishing, hb, 137pp; pdf supplied by publisher). He is invited by Frank Lunt to Gulshaw, a run-down seaside town, to collect the series, which includes such titles as *Of Humanity as Chrysalis, Of the World as Lair, On the Purposes of Night,* and *Of the Uses of the Dead.* (You can probably guess where this is going.) But Lunt has just one volume, and directs Fairman to the possessor of the next, and so it goes. Reading each of the books brings on strange thoughts and visions, and Fairman becomes desperate to leave this strange, damp, sticky little town. But everyone seems awfully pleased to have him there, and as they say: "there is so much more to see". Or is it that there's so much more to sea?

Fans of Lovecraft will regard it as a treat to have a writer of Campbell's stature producing a short novel in this vein, and it provides many eerie images and scenes; anyone who has seen a British beach studded with jellyfish can imagine the kind of horrors described here. The idea of a seedy seaside town that drops its human facade in the off-season is creepily believable. ("He could have thought the town was not so much resting from its summer labours as reverting to its ordinary state.") As Fairman finds himself stuck there for an extra day, and another day, and another, while his wife gets annoyed and his boss on his back, it's hard not to empathise – though he's given so many good reasons to run for his life that you can't help wondering why he doesn't.

And that was the problem for me, that the too-frequent hints about what's going on were too knowing, too nudge-nudge wink-wink, to be truly frightening: for example hands are "glistening" and "soft and moist", handshakes are "damp and pliable", palms are "clammy" and "yielded so much". The chthonic innuendo wears a bit thin, and even begins to feel like fan service. Fairman works so hard to ignore or rationalise everything he sees ("Of course the people were wearing plastic beach shoes, which made their feet look translucent and swollen") that the reader's eyes begin to roll. Loving pastiche comes close to tipping into presumably unintentional parody.

More positively, the book is so perfectly suited to cinematic adaptation that one wouldn't be surprised to learn it began life as a film treatment. The role of Fairman would be ideal for Daniel Radcliffe or Dominic West, and a version of this produced to the same standard as *The Woman in Black* or *The Awakening* might give us, at last, a definitive mythos film. If this had been the first Lovecraftian story I'd ever read, I would have loved it – as I did Brian Lumley's *The Burrowers Beneath*, back in my schooldays. As it is, I enjoyed it, but I'd hoped to enjoy it much more. Still, I've often found that horror stories continue to grow in my estimation long after I've read them, as the scariest parts fester, and that might well be the case here. The climactic scene in the Church of the First Word is magnificent, and the book is worth reading for that sequence alone.

---

## Live_Transmission: Joy Division Reworked
*Reviewed by Stephen Theaker*

The publicity material for **Live_Transmission: Joy Division Reworked** (The Symphony Hall, Birmingham, 28 September 2013), performed by Scanner and The Heritage Orchestra, made it clear that one should not expect a Joy Division covers band, a niche well served already by Peter Hook and the Light. However, what it did not make clear was that these were not, on the whole, Joy Division songs at all, but rather entirely new pieces vaguely inspired by Joy Division songs. From time to time the slightly repetitive short films that illustrated the performance (for example by moving through cross-sections of the human body or showing space invaders fighting over the pattern from the *Unknown Pleasures* cover) would display snatches of lyrics, which was fortunate because otherwise listeners would rarely have had any idea which songs were theoretically being reworked.

But it began quite promisingly, with a building swell of white noise and light that burst at last into a thudding, percussive take on "Transmission", the bassline and drums used to drive a Krautrockish instrumental version. But it went on a bit too long, and there was (as was the case for most of the concert) no sign of anyone singing the song. A few snatched samples were pretty much all we got in that line, aside from a closing performance of "Love Will Tear Us Apart" (over apparently random orchestral playing) that left you wishing for Paul Young. Unfortunately that take on "Transmission" was the concert's high point for me, as from then on the Joy Division elements of the performance became ever harder to discern.

Other songs performed included (I think), "She's Lost Control", "Isolation" and "Dead Souls", but billing the concert as Kraftwerk, Bowie or Hans Zimmer reworked would have been almost equally plausible, given the scarcity of obvious links to the originals. Since watching the concert I've read interviews with the performers, who stressed their desire to avoid being a "crass tribute act", and that's a reasonable goal, and I'm sure there are subtle connections to the original songs that were difficult to spot on a first listen, but it's being sold as Joy Division: Reworked, not as original avant garde pieces. I did try to take it on its own terms, but as avant garde music it felt uninspired and unchallenging, putting me in mind of nothing so much as the ambient remixes of Moby's cover versions played loudly.

More positively, the players were well-rehearsed, the performance going without any apparent hitches, and it was all appropriately moody and atmospheric (so dark in fact that we could rarely see the performers). There have been tweets from other attendees who thought it was wonderful, though in some cases even they note the high numbers of people dashing off to the bar. If these compositions are released as an album, I'll probably grow to like it. Perhaps if I'd had a chance to get to know the music first, or if I'd been able to see what the musicians were doing, I might have enjoyed the performance more. Even now, though I remember being unimpressed and rather bored during the concert, there's a part of me thinking, Joy Division songs, ripped up, remixed and played by an orchestra in the Symphony Hall: that sounds great. So why was it so dull?

---

# Nexus Omnibus, Vol. 2
*Reviewed by Stephen Theaker*

**Nexus Omnibus, Vol. 2** (Dark Horse, ebook, 423pp; Dark Horse app purchase), written by Mike Baron with most artwork by Steve Rude, collects issues 12 to 25 of the original series from First Comics. They continue the comic's odd mix of high seriousness and low humour. The former: the punishment of genocidal maniacs, as super-powered Nexus puts to death the mass murderers of whom he mysteriously dreams. An example of the latter: the ongoing adventures of Clonezone the Hilariator, a terrible Catskills-style comedian who travels the galaxy from one crummy gig to another, always in hope of making it big.

In this volume the main storyline goes in a number of interesting directions. The dreams get too much for Nexus and he has surgery to blank them out, leading to him live like the guys from *Men Behaving Badly*, only with more smashing of televisions and accidental deaths. Nexus's girlfriend gets fed up with him and leaves their home planet Ylum to establish a spaceship factory on Mars. When Nexus's powers are finally restored, his nightmares will bring him to our own solar system.

I wish I could have read this book in Comixology's app.

Dark Horse do deserve respect for not joining the rush to hand the entire comics industry over to one distributor, but using their apps is a struggle. The iPad app crashes if the device isn't connected to the internet, it took months for this purchase to show up on there, and even then the app couldn't complete the download without crashing. The Android app downloaded the book, but the guided panel view is unhelpful, an unnecessarily huge swipe is required to turn the page, there are no options for blanking out the panels not currently focused on, and it hangs for a second before flipping.

Despite those off-putting problems, I enjoyed the book. Mike Baron's writing here has a sour flavour, seeming to find its source in anger and frustration rather than joy or pleasure, but that gives it a unique feel. It's a book about consequences, whether it's Nexus giving retribution for almost-forgotten sins, or the surviving children of his victims vowing to seek out and punish him in their turn, and as consequences accumulate it becomes very grim. The bursts of zany humour didn't click with me at all, especially when mixed with stories featuring murder and abuse. The book's biggest flaw is the interpolation of the painfully unfunny Tales from the Clonezone backup strip, which breaks the more consistent mood of the Nexus adventures. Getting through its eight pages was never anything less than a trial, nobly endured to reach the next episode of Nexus.

The artwork is where the book shines. The stylish pencils on the main strip are by Steve Rude, with inks by Eric Shanower and John Nyberg, while Shanower, Mark A. Nelson, Hilary Barta and Keith Giffen pencil backups and fill-ins. Despite the many hands at work, the style is consistent, striking page and panel design always a major feature. Perspectives constantly change and aliens look truly bizarre. Artistry is evident on every page, not least in Les Dorscheid's subtly shaded colours; the Marvel and DC colouring of the period looks rudimentary in comparison.

Overall, recommended, but buy it in print – not often

you'll hear me say that! – and skip the Clonezone stories till you've read the rest. They rarely feed back into the Nexus stories, and you'll resent them much less as an extra.

---

## Star Trek: Titan #1: Taking Wing
*Reviewed by Stephen Theaker*

The idea of a novel series putting William Riker in command of his own starship is very appealing. The guy deserves it. However, **Star Trek: Titan #1: Taking Wing** by Michael A. Martin and Andy Mangels (Pocket books, ebook, 5700ll; Kindle purchase), first in the *Star Trek: Titan* series, does him no justice. It begins during the events of the painfully dull and frustrating *Star Trek: Nemesis*, which perhaps explains why it took me eight years to read more than the first few pages. Poor old Spock is shown to be still stuck in hiding on Romulus – where he was parked in the *Next Generation* two-parter "Reunification" – when Tom Hardy makes his bid for power.

Leaving him among the chaos, we travel to Captain Riker, touring his new ship, excitingly the most species-diverse the Federation has ever seen. The ship's doctor sounds like the result of a facehugger infecting a dinosaur, the astrophysicist is from a zero-G world, and another crew member requires an aquatic cabin. But that's about as exciting as it gets, bar a prison breakout and a quick space battle towards the end. The tour over, the ship is soon sent off on a diplomatic mission to Romulus, where various factions, including the Remans, are battling for supremacy now that Hardy's moved on to better roles.

The *Titan*'s mission is to make sure nothing interesting happens.

The problem of Star Trek in its later years has been in finding new chunks of space to explore: the other side of DS9's wormhole, *Voyager* in the Delta Quadrant, the Thallonian Empire of Peter David's New Frontier series. *Star Trek: Enterprise* felt like it was pottering about in the

Vulcans' backyard. The new films give up on that and settle for making the most of established locations. In theory, *Star Trek: Titan* has the widest of open roads ahead, the future of the Trek universe, but it's too bogged down in continuity to fully explore it.

Everything's already been decided, little can be changed, and we're left with a talky adventure that only highlights the sense of narrative exhaustion in the Trek universe, a universe that was once about the three Fs – fighting, f\*\*king and thinking – but was by *Nemesis* a succession of meetings around a desk, a tradition ignobly continued here. No wonder there are hardcore Trek fans who hate the new films: with every shining, sexy frame they show how badly astray the franchise had gone.

Many of the crew members here seem to be from various television episodes and spin-off novels; I'm not enough of a fan to always know which ones, my Trek encyclopaedia is out of date and I couldn't be bothered to look them up online. But though the book isn't considerate enough to give us a footnote or two explaining the sources, it gets constantly bogged down in making sure the reader knows the ins and outs of their life stories. Anything that has ever happened to the character seems to get a reference, all of which would have been better left to be revealed when other characters showed an interest.

It's a tedious, self-parodic book, no character apparently able to utter a line without it being bracketed by sentences explaining exactly what they meant by what they said, how they feel about it, or how they think the person they are talking to might take it. This reaches its nadir in conversations involving Deanna Troi, still gamely trying to show that a shoulder to cry on is the most important component of a starship. After a Romulan says "[Y]ou are a liar or a fool, human. Which is it?" to a Starfleet admiral, we learn that "Deanna felt haughtiness, with a sprinkling of surprise". Thanks for that, Deanna.

So why did I read it to the end, even when I had much

better books on the go? Well, it was on the Kindle and I was supposed to be reading a paper book and however good the paper book I always drift away, and here's where I drifted. (Technically the ebook is fine, but Kindle use is restricted to four devices; annoying if you like to read on whatever device is closest to hand.) And it's Riker and Troi: however dull the adventure I'm interested in what's happening to them. Another thing I liked was that it seems to establish (though maybe it was already established elsewhere and I've forgotten) that Tuvok was the guy who looked a lot like Tuvok on the bridge of Captain Sulu's ship in *Star Trek VI*. That was nice.

I'm sure that there are good *Star Trek* novels written by people other than James Blish, Peter David and Alan Dean Foster, but this isn't one of them.

---

# The Unsettled Dust and Other Stories
*Reviewed by Stephen Theaker*

As far as I know, **The Unsettled Dust and Other Stories** by Robert Aickman (Audible, digital audiobook, 8 hrs 37 mins; supplied by publisher) has been my first taste of this writer's work. He is of course very well regarded in horror circles, and has long been on my to-read-at-some-point list. I wasn't disappointed.

The narrator of this edition, published by Audible themselves, is Reece Shearsmith of The League of Gentlemen. The recording is very clear. There are no sound effects or music, but their absence feels appropriate. His reading is splendid, aside from a couple of tiny fluffs.

In "The Unsettled Dust" (90 mins) he manages to find exactly the right tone to convey the stuffiness and dullness of its protagonist, Mr Oxenhope, without boring the listener; a clever trick. In that story Oxenhope tells us of his peculiar experiences while acting as the agent of a fund rather like the National Heritage. He is sent to a dusty old manor house in which two sisters live, and he becomes enamoured of one of them.

"The Houses of the Russians" is a creepy story about a property man looking for a good investment to bring a big fish; his evening walk takes him to an area where there are strange parties going on in every house. "No Stronger Than a Flower" is a warning to spouses tempted to badger their partners into changing, and in "The Cicerones" a solitary artist has a peculiar experience in a Belgian church. "The Next Glade", one of five stories longer than an hour, introduces us to a bored housewife whose interest in extramarital diversions leads to trouble for her and her husband.

"Ravissante", after a lengthy preamble discussing an awkward friendship, moves on to an artist's account of his visit to the house of a elderly lady who gives him the willies, yet seems to be able to control him. "Bind Your Hair" concerns a woman struggling to resign herself to a very sensible marriage, who against all expectation goes out for a long walk on her own and meets a pair of odd children, their pigs and a very odd lady. The last story is the longest, "The Stains", another steadily horrible story of a man who tries to settle with an unsuitable woman.

The stories all take their time, and never try too hard, having a take-it-or-leave-it attitude that is very dignified. They don't try to knock you off your perch with cheap scares, but instead leave you wondering whether your apparently solid perch might actually be quite rotten. That subtlety and patience was admirable, even if my preference is more for writers who push the weirdness a little further, and don't allow the dullness of the protagonists to set the pace of the stories to *quite* such an extent.

I found the audiobook best suited to headphones, its quiet, undemonstrative narration too easy to tune out with passive, ambient listening, and I'm sure that in the course of the book's eight hours I missed several important details. It is worth allowing a period between each story, lest the protagonists run into one.

They tend to be drawn from the same well: men who would be better off avoiding marital entanglements, and less frequently the women who have become entangled with them. The theme, that women really are quite a bother, dates the book somewhat, since men who find women and their ways such a terrible nuisance are no longer required to marry them, but I still found myself gripped by the stories whenever they had my undivided attention.

## We See a Different Frontier
*Reviewed by Stephen Theaker*

**We See a Different Frontier** (The Future Fire, ebook, 3447ll; Kindle purchase), edited by Fabio Fernandes and Djibril al-Ayad, is an anthology of sixteen stories, and also a special issue of the magazine *The Future Fire*, which publishes fantasy work with a political edge. After a year's hiatus, the magazine encouraged applications from potential guest editors. That led first to *Outlaw Bodies*, edited by Lori Selke, and now to this book. The submission guidelines set an interesting challenge: to approach science fiction from the point of view not of those pushing the frontier out, in their wagon trains to the stars, but from the perspective of those who have experienced the expanding frontier from the other side. When I read the guidelines, my thoughts went towards the alien experience of human expansion, but the introduction makes it clear that the editors were more interested in "*us*, the aliens from Earth. Foreigners. Strangers to the current dominant culture." And so only a few of the stories are set in space, most being set here on Earth, using science fiction to address historical, contemporary and controversial issues directly, rather than retreating to the safe Star Trekkian distance of metaphorical alien planets.

But those stories that feature aliens use them well. In "Them Ships" Silvia Moreno-Garcia considers how the flattening of human social structures by an alien invasion might not be entirely unwelcome among those currently at the bottom of the pile. A spacecraft hangs over the city in "A Bridge of Words" by Dinesh Rao, broadcasting an incomprehensible message, while Riya researches the tattoos of the country she left behind. Both are good stories, but Sunny Moraine's "A Heap of Broken Images" is astonishing. It's the heartbreaking story of an alien guide showing insensitive human tourists around the scene of a massacre. The story's point is made by how unsurprised the reader is to learn what happened.

"What Really Happened in Ficandula" by Rochita Loenen-Ruiz is the only other story to take us off-world. It begins with a strong taste of *Battlestar Galactica*, as Gemma's ship arrives at New Cordillera after six hundred and twenty leaps to throw off their pursuers, but it develops very quickly into a fine story with its own flavour that draws on the kind of shameful incidents that go hand in hand with imperial power and colonisation: forced migration, forced adoption, trigger-happy soldiers.

Some stories show us the survivors of global catastrophes, such as Joyce Chng's "Lotus", which shows people surviving in a waterlogged land, who find a wonderful source of fresh water and must decide whether to claim ownership of it, given all the consequences that defending it might bring. "Fleet" by Sandra McDonald is the story of a girl called Bridge who used to be a boy named Magahet Joseph Howard USN. She's married to a man whose other wife hopes she'll "be gored to death by a goonie pig". Bridge's people live on an island which was once part of an empire, and isn't any more, and they have mixed feelings about re-establishing contact with whatever's left of civilisation.

Shweta Narayan's "The Arrangement of Their Parts" is set in 1665, where an Englishman is trying to exploit clockwork life forms, while "Forests of the Night" by Gabriel Murray is told by the unacknowledged son of an English captain, who brings him back to England from Kuala Lumpur. The mother is left behind, the boy employed as a valet.

Something is killing sheep, horses and then men, and it needs to be hunted. Though they're not writers one would expect to meet at this party, Kipling and Doyle came to mind, and the story isn't embarrassed by the comparison. "Pancho Villa's Flying Circus" by Ernest Hogan sees Tesla creating a helicopter-borne death ray for Mexican revolutionaries, only for it to be hijacked by a guy angry about Hollywood's cultural appropriation of his girlfriend. It's the kind of pulpy cartoon story with a serious theme that would fit neatly into an Obverse anthology. "I Stole the D.C.'s Eyeglass" is about a girl who worries for her stubborn sister, Minisare, who disappears off into the forest and doesn't want to be given a husband. Sofia Samatar shows a community ruined by commercial exploitation, so used to the roar of machinery that the children can all read lips – but it ends on a hopeful note.

Lavie Tidhar is one of my favourite writers at the moment and "Dark Continents" is another excellent story from him. "We began to edit, but we were sloppy at first", we read. That process created a new role for Livingstone, an African invasion of the confederacy, a Jewish homeland in Uganda. Style, ideas, storytelling: Tidhar's stories excel in every area. A sentence here sums up the injustice of colonialism: "We had moved en masse to this land, empty but for its people, granted to us by the power of British empire and its King and parliament."

Another of my favourite stories in the anthology was "Old Domes" by J.Y. Yang. Jing-Li is a cullmaster of buildings: when they are to be knocked down or refurbished she must clear the way by killing their guardian spirits. The story looks not just at the ongoing after-effects of colonialism, but also at the histories lost as colonial powers impose a new year zero. And it also has some good fights! "How to Make a Time Machine Do Things that Are Not in the Manual or The Gambiarra Method" is a Rudy Ruckerish story by Fabio Fernandes about researchers who discover time travel "during experiments on locative media and augmented reality as applied to elevators". This makes sense, since even ordinary lifts are known to cause time dilations. "Droplet" by Rahul Kanakia inverts the usual story of the Indian emigrant who agonises over having taken their skills abroad – see for example the film *Swades* – to show what happens when they return to India, in this case because the USA has begun to dry up.

"Vector" is a cyberpunk story told in the second person by Benjanun Sriduangkaew: "You. Are. (A weapon. A virus. A commandment from God.)" You are literally plugged into the internet, and the hope is that you'll do something to reverse the exploitation of your country and the steam-rolling of its culture, a recurring theme in the book: "This is how to rewrite a country's past, and when a past is gone it is easy to replace the present with convenience." Similar themes are explored in "Remembering Turinam" by N.A. Ratnayake, despite its more historical (or fantastical?) setting. This wasn't my favourite of the stories here, its protagonist Salai a bit too self-righteous and unpleasant to carry the reader. The story is essentially a conversation, the subject the active erasing of the Turian language by the Rytari invaders, and the question of whether it should be restored, and if so how. An exploration of the viral nature of language might have been very interesting in this context – you can't keep a good word down! – but language is a topic big enough to inspire an anthology in itself, and a story shouldn't be blamed for not exploring every angle.

The book was hardly published in hopes of a pat on the head from a white Englishman, and even the act of reviewing it – issuing my judgment upon the hard work of these plucky foreign types! – seems to go against the spirit of the book. The afterword by Ekaterina Sedia is a more sensitive response to the book's themes than I could ever write (though if I had thought like her that the stories shared an anti-scientific theme I would have seen it as a weakness rather than a strength). But, for what my opinion is worth, I thought the book was absolutely terrific. The short length of the stories meant none had time to waste, and there is a great deal of variety. It's full of surprising plots and perspectives, and if the premise of the book might make you expect a lecture, don't think of the finger-wagging kind, think more of an inspirational guest speaker who opens your eyes to new ideas and new approaches. Many anthologists, when asked about the lack of diversity in their work, declare that they care about quality and not quotas. This book shows that diversity needn't come at a cost, and is in fact an extremely valuable quality for an anthology.

On the technical side, the Kindle edition is fine, apart from (on my devices, at least) being set in block paragraphs with a line space between. That could be a deliberate choice – it does look rather elegant – but it means more page turns, especially on smaller screens. Other than that, the book is very highly recommended.

---

## Also Received, But Not Yet Reviewed
*Notes by Stephen Theaker*

Adaf, Shimon, *Sunburnt Faces* (PS Publishing): described by Lavie Tidhar as "probably the most important fantastical novel of the year".

Adams, Guy, *The Clown Service** (Del Rey)

Alexander, Rebecca, *The Secrets of Life and Death** (Del Rey): I like the shape of this book. It's a hardback, but in a similar ratio to the paperbacks of Livre de Poche.

Campbell, Ramsey, *The Pretence* (PS Publishing): a novella.

Clemens, Brian, *Rabbit Pie* (PS Publishing): a collection of short stories from the Avengers man, with an introduction from Stephen Gallagher.

Connell, Brendan, *Miss Homicide Plays the Flute* (Eibonvale Press)

Dunn, Robin Wyatt, *My Name Is Dee* (John Ott)

Ford, Richard, *The Shattered Crown* (Headline)

Gresh, Lois H. (ed.), *Dark Fusions: Where Monsters Lurk!*

(PS Publishing): includes stories by Darrell Schweitzer, Lisa Morton, Nick Cato, Yvonne Navarro and others.

Harris, Joe, Michael Walsh and others, *The X-Files, Season 10, Vol. 1* (IDW)

Harvey, Edwina (ed.), *Andromeda Spaceways Inflight Magazine #58*: includes Jacob Edwards' review of *Sharps* by K.J. Parker.

Hurley, Kameron, *God's War** (Del Rey)

Matheson, Richard Christian, *The Ritual of Illusion* (PS Publishing)

Olson, Danel (ed.), *Exotic Gothic 5, Volume I* (PS Publishing): includes work by Joyce Carol Oates, Anna Taborska, Nancy A. Collins and others.

Olson, Danel (ed.), *Exotic Gothic 5, Volume II* (PS Publishing): includes work by Thana Niveau, Reggie Oliver, Lucy Taylor and others.

Perryman, Neil, *Adventures with the Wife in Space* (Faber and Faber)

Polansky, Daniel, *She Who Waits** (Hodder & Stoughton): the third book in the Low Town series.

Richards, Justin, *The Suicide Exhibition* (Del Rey): book one of the Never War.

Tubb, E.C., *The Winds of Gath* (Wildside Press): audiobook, read by Rish Outfield.

---

Expect **Theaker's Quarterly Fiction #47** at the end of March 2014. Deadline for subs is 28 February 2014.

Most weeks begin with a new review on our blog:
**www.theakersquarterly.blogspot.com**

Stephen is effortlessly annoying on Twitter:
**www.twitter.com/Rolnikov**

Our email address is:
**theakersquarterlyfiction@gmail.com**

www.ingramcontent.com/pod-product-compliance
Lightning Source LLC
Chambersburg PA
CBHW060626130626
46555CB00002B/676